FRENZY OF DESIRE

FRENZY OF DESIRE

JOHN B. THOMPSON

CUTTING EDGE

ISBN-13: 978-1-957868-95-0

Published by
Cutting Edge Books
PO Box 8212
Calabasas, CA 91372
www.cuttingedgebooks.com

Love is blind,
And lovers cannot see
The pretty follies
That themselves commit.
　　　—*The Merchant of Venice*

FRENZY OF DESIRE

CHAPTER ONE

WITH feverish haste Laurent Dennison stripped off her clothes and stood before the mirror, nude, her body aglow with a patrician symmetry that was relieved and enrichened by the elegance of its structure, the snowy translucence of her flawless skin and fabulous coloring of her hair, lips, the peaks of her upthrust breasts, and the slightly tanned calves that seemed turned from some fabulous stone.

She stood sideways and noted with satisfaction the full creamy cones of her breasts, still undaunted and without even the suggestion of a droop. A shuddering sigh of relief went through her and feeling much better, poured scotch into a glass and added a little soda. She sat on the side of her bed and still reflected in the mirror looked at her image and thought hard.

Why was she unhappy? She had money, clothes, and every material wish could be granted. She could merely by the tilt of a dark eyebrow make men fall over themselves for her favors. She shuddered, hugging herself as a tide of lasciviousness throbbed through her loins and brought sweat to her brow. That was one thing. She always hated herself after giving herself to a man, a matter she wondered at because she always enjoyed it. A sickening longing ached in her stomach ... how I enjoyed it ... how I wish ... She shook her hair over her shoulders and fell backward on the bed, the lines of her body arched in a gentle curve that threw her breasts into prominence and accentuated the delightful curve of her thighs.

Her thoughts went back to what had just transpired a few minutes before.

The big sinewy man seated opposite her in a deep maroon nub chair was relaxed but his eyes were hard and all seeing and the twist of his mouth indicated saturnine disapproval.

"Laurent Dennison, the girl who is so happy that she can't contain herself, who has all the money there is, who is going to do everything there is to do, and taste everything that makes an impression on the senses."

Her laughing face went so suddenly serious that it was almost audible. "I didn't ask you here to be sarcastic, Dan."

"Exactly why did you ask me here? I'm a busy man, my time is about as finely divided as it can be and still allow me four hours sleep taken at odd times in odd places."

She smiled a little alcoholically. "Not every girl is lucky enough to have a doctor who was once in love with her."

He shrugged. "You keep telling yourself that. Suppose I told you you made love very badly because you were too intent on being loved, that you've been a spoiled brat all your life and needed a switching the worst way?"

"I'd say you were trying to get a raise out of me. Wasn't I young enough and beautiful enough to compensate for my lack of experience?"

He nodded. "Somewhat. There was also my professorial out-look. You learned a lot while under my tutelage."

"Have another drink, Dan."

"Thanks, no. One was too many. Now I'll have to chew all sorts of revolting muck to get the odor out of my mouth. I have an operation in two hours. What was it you wanted?"

"I wanted to talk about myself, out now I feel too good to talk about me. Maybe it's the drinks."

"You've had enough of them to know." He shifted his lean bulk in his chair. "Larry, you're not being very smart about this life you lead. You're not happy and you know it."

Her face lengthened a little. "Yes, Dan, I know it. I know it even now when I'm drunk and feel like a million."

His smile was sardonic. "You show rare flashes of intelligence."

Her big grey eyes filled with tears which she dashed away with the backs of her hands. "But what shall I do?" She shook her head making her dark soft hair dance about her shoulders. "I'm not drunk any more and I know I've got to do something. I'm at a dead end and I'm ..." She shuddered. "I'm going crazy ... stark raving crazy. I can't even get up in the morning without the horrors, then I reach for the bottle."

"Which," he said offensively, "will one day make a witch out of you. You, the most alive and beautiful woman I've ever seen ... a witch. Your gums will get purple and draw away from your teeth; your face will become a map of Mars; your skin will dry up like weathered parchment and the bones will begin to stick out. Worse yet, your breasts, the most beautiful part of you will become lax and fall to your waist like fat bologna links."

"Shut up!" She leaped to her feet, her body quivering in the sheath of a dress that spoke silently, but plainly, of the money she spent for clothes. "You're saying that to infuriate me. My breasts ill never fall ... *Never*, do you hear?"

"Very dramatic," he said with a smirk. "And very indicative of the small rat of fear that the truth always starts to gnawing on you. Do you have the guts to take yourself in hand or will you wind up screaming and gibbering in a wet sheet or a strait jacket?"

She collapsed on the couch, bouncing on its elegant grey upholstery, weeping loudly and wetly.

He stood up, long, distinguished and unmoved by her stormy tears. "Better think it over, pet, and if you still think I'm in love with you I'd advise a re-estimate. I'm not going to advise you, because I'm too well acquainted with that goat headed obstinacy with which you're so heavily steeped. You'll get yourself in hand or you'll crack up. In either case I doubt that I'd be of a lot of help. If you get sick call me again. When you want to talk get someone else. My time is too valuable."

He left her huddled miserably on the couch, her curves distorted but still lovely, jerking occasionally to the impetus of a sob.

She sat on the silk-covered stool before her dressing mirrors and began to stroke a brush through her hair, making it so softly unmanageable that it seemed to crawl about her head. The fire in her loins seemed to leap and sear her as she struggled with her briefs, the bare act of putting them on sending a weakening shock through her limbs. She smoothed a few tiny wrinkles from them and turned to look at the lacquered white gesture about her middle, shivering a little with narcissistic delight. She snapped on a bra of thin nylon net that served as unneeded support, making her breasts seem pinker, their tips darker. She bent over and cuddled them a few times to assure a complete, unbinding fit, then slipped a white tricot half slip over her hips and adjusted it.

She whirled, making the slip rise almost to waist height, then stopped and watched as it settled down again obscuring the strong columns of her thighs. The night was warm so she selected a dress of striped cotton that, on her, acquired a kind of divinity.

"Please don't put it on."

Larry spun around, a little bleat of fright coming from her throat. "Oh ... My God, Elsie Denton, what are you doing here?"

"I came ..." Elsie made a helpless gesture with her hands. "I came ..." Her voice dropped in humility. "Because I couldn't help myself."

"You nearly scared me to death. Where have you been?"

"In the bathroom."

Larry's eyes narrowed as she considered the girl. They had met some time ago at the Country Club tennis courts and Larry had been appalled at the swift sureness of the girl's game. She was poison on the courts and good looking too. There was a certain masculinity about her but she wasn't too muscular, her face was well featured and she wore her hair in an attractive poodle cut. Her breasts were small but assertive, and Larry was now treated to a mild shock. She was hard to shock because she knew too much about such people, but so far it had never touched her, personally.

"Please don't make me go, Larry," the girl pleaded, her pretty brown eyes aswim with tears.

Larry felt sorry for her. "I won't, dear. What about a drink? I'm about half loaded now."

"Please ... make it large and strong."

They sat in the living room on the couch and sipped their drinks for a moment in silence then Larry said, "Elsie, I'm not a fool and I can see a lot of things now I hadn't been able to see before. I know why you're here; but I must admit it is a surprise."

"Then you don't hate me?"

"Of course not. I'm not a simpleton. I know about such things."

Elsie bent over slowly and kissed her hand where it lay on the couch, the touch of the girl's lips sending a peculiar twit of excitement through her and again her need for sensuous gratification started storming at her.

"Thank you," said Elsie, her eyes wet again. "You don't know how relieved I am. I just had to see you naked ... I *had* to. You're the most beautiful woman I ever saw."

"How long have you been this way, Elsie?"

The girl shook her head. "I don't know. I always played with boys and didn't care for girls at all until I grew up. Then I went off to boarding school and there was a girl ..." She forced her lips into a straight line. She sighed and toyed with her glass then emptied it. "May I have another?"

"Certainly." She fixed her another drink as well as one for herself.

"Larry, I know you'll find this hard to believe, but I love you. I've loved you since that day we first met."

"Tell me, Elsie, do you really mean you love me like a man loves a woman?"

"Yes, I think so. I want to hold you and kiss you and fondle you. I wanted to see you undressed so badly, that it became an obsession. I want to protect you and do things for you ... I'm like that."

"But, dear, I need no protection."

"I know you don't, but that's the way I feel."

Larry, feeling the excitement rise within her, leaned backward on the arm of the couch and stretched. Her breasts lifted, their eager heads straining against the frail bra and the slip slid upward, giving Elsie a look at the triumphant swells of her thighs and a wispy glimpse of her misty white briefs that couldn't conceal the darkness they covered.

Larry was a little more than drunk. Elsie was also a little drunk and almost in a frenzy at the sight before her. With a throaty moan she bent forward and kissed the nearest thigh holding it with a reverence that Larry could sense, if not see.

Larry suppressed a cry of something akin to fright as her leg seemed to go dead from the paralytic response of her nerves that flared hotly for a second, then paled to a passive rhythmic flicker.

Elsie sat up and buried her face in her hands. "You're so lovely ... so lovely ... so lovely."

Larry sat up jerkily and tried to stem the awful surges of response the touch had initiated, her eyes half seeing and her lips parted. Elsie took her hands down and looked at her hard ... and seeing no resentment became bolder. Larry's eyes held that look of dazed expectancy that Elsie had seen before and her heart pounded wildly ...

"Please Elsie ... don't ... don't. I can't, really I can't. It'd ..."

CHAPTER TWO

FOR a month Dan Weatherby held his peace. Although he was definitely not in love with Larry he did have a strong affection for her and a great deal of his hard front, when talking to her, was affected with a purpose in mind. She was without parents and knowing the need for a strong, if not overtly outspoken shoulder, he chose to provide it.

Finally, after the third mutual acquaintance had repeated the information that Elsie Denton had moved in with Larry, he stole some time from his hospital calls one night and paid her a visit.

The door was ajar so he didn't knock, but pushed it open to surprise Larry and Elsie standing before a mirror.

A grim smile touched his lips. "Miss Denton, I sit in judgment over no man or woman regarding their morals, but what I have to say to Larry will not be very pleasant to your ears; therefore, I'd suggest you go drink a short beer or something that will occupy you for a time."

"I'm not going a step," flared Elsie, stamping her foot, her face flaming with shame. "And you're not going to do a thing to Larry."

"If that is to be your attitude," he said calmly with a perceptible ring of steel in his voice, "I withdraw my *suggestion*. Get out and don't come back until I leave. Is that clear?"

She gasped as though he had slapped her, but her will was no match for the steady grey eyes of the doctor, so with a half sob she turned and ran from the room.

He sighed and took a chair and watched the blood gradually recede from Larry's face.

They sat and looked at each other for some time until finally Larry's face reddened again and she burst out. "All right, go ahead and say it, dammit."

Dan built a steeple of his long fingers and squinted at them absently. "I hardly know what to say, really. I refuse to crawl down the mean level of outraged mediocrity. My science tells me that what you have been doing is not necessarily as bad as it might sound or appear. On the other hand, science speaks guardedly and qualifies what it says. It cannot be expected to know what your background is and what's going on inside you. I have reason to doubt that you're getting off entirely unscathed. I doubt if anything a human does makes a lot of sinful difference if the principal isn't aware of the sin. It could just as easily be a sin for a child to suck a thumb, but since the child is happily unaware of sin he goes blithely on his way sucking at will. You, on the other hand probably suffer from remorse. Should the day ever come when Miss Denton uncovers some latent streak of … ummm, peculiarity, shall we say, in you and you find it impossible or repugnant to be with a man, then I shudder to think of what you'd think of yourself."

She went pale. "Dan … tell me, is that possible?"

"I don't know. I know what I have been taught as a doctor. I read my journals and I attend short courses. I still don't know everything. No one does. I mentioned a possibility."

"Then it could happen?"

"It most assuredly could. It has. The man in me dictates that I should rant and rave about the moral aspect of this strange enchantment. I refuse to do so. I can, therefore, only point out these things. Your friends all know about it. Their reactions, as you might guess, are mixed. Your name is being pitched hither and thither, gathering no small amount of tar ... which, of course, leaves you quite cold and unconcerned. That's the attitude you'd naturally take. What you felt need not be, and most likely isn't, one and the same. I dare say the first time with Elsie was at a moment when you needed a man badly. She was fortuitous, she was novel and for that reason, highly satisfactory.

"I believe you have, in a sense, transferred a considerable portion of the responsibility to her shoulders, escaping, thereby, a lot of pillow punching, sleepless nights. A neat maneuver all right, but when you get like that you've taken the first step toward the habit of shrugging off responsibility and after a time it becomes very easy to do so. You have kidded yourself so well that it has become habituated. You're not much good to anyone, least of all, yourself."

She looked at him through enigmatic eyes. "You know, you've made better sense tonight than you ever have before."

"That any of it stuck causes me to pause and wonder."

She got up and walked to a sideboard and made a drink for herself. "Drinking this evening?"

"Thanks, no."

He reflected as she stood there that her grey pleated orlon skirt was as full of delectable hips as the burgundy silk blouse was full of delectable chest. Whatever turmoil was in her mind, whatever lack of direction and whatever boredom had done to her outlook, nothing had been able to mar the superb perfection of her body or distort its classic proportions. She turned around and surprised him looking at her, but he was unperturbed.

"So I still excite you?"

"If I ever seemed to imply that I was unmoved by a beautiful woman, please forget it. I'm not dead and I can still make you cry uncle."

She took a deep pull at her drink, put it down and slid into his lap. "Bet you couldn't."

For a moment he remained taut and unresponsive, then he bent his head and kissed her. She slid her arms around his neck and released the pent-up need for a man that had been plaguing her subconsciously ever since she had accepted Elsie into her life. The need must have a voice and found one in the throaty eager note that found egress difficult because of the pressure of their lips. Her skirt, being soft and easily moved, slid upward from her efforts to bring her body into the closest proximity with his; and her thighs glowed softly in the dim overhead light. When his hands found them she thought she'd faint and their old life came back and unrolled swiftly before her. The laughing easy manner of his that always grew serious when their love became heated. The delicate and long drawn out roving of his long fingers ... fingers that were playing a silent but lovely melody on the fine skin of her thighs, climbing with a slowness that made her shudder and clench him tighter, climbing with a deft sureness that Larry knew would soon climb no higher. They were now wandering about like blind moles searching their way through a labyrinth ... but she knew they weren't blind. Her body went hard in breathless anticipation, scorching tongues of sensation blistering her in repeated waves.

Her lips were free now and wide to admit her gasping breath, but he still clung to first one, then the other, playing with them as his fingers seared her inner-being, sending two tides from opposite directions, shaking her sorely.

The blind suddenly could see and a frail obstacle was an obstacle no more. Her long, red lacquered nails stung him. She was bared to the waist now, the wonder of her middle obscured benevolently and excitingly by a breath of white tricot through which her skin showed pinkly and now her throat seemed bursting with an unspoken poem set to strange music of such ecstasy as is never heard under different circumstances.

"Dan … please hurry … please hurry. I still love you, Dan … I always have, but I forget, except at times … Oh … Dan … times like these. Love me hard, Dan … make me beg you to stop … make me cry and whimper, then make me scream … I can't stand much more … more … much more!"

He let his hands wander down her back while her starving lips searched hungrily for his, found them and became a part of him clinging, moving, her hair tumbled and disordered. His hands maneuvered filling themselves with hot flesh, tender and so smooth that his mind reeled, losing a previously avowed intent, forcing her closer and closer until she gasped for breath.

Clothes fell to the floor, forming pools of nylon, cotton, and wool at their feet. The soft carpet received them and her body went into exhorbitant action, powerful, demanding, objective as an infant's mouth.

"It was … always this way … always. Heaven … reach me … reach me." She swallowed noisily and she urged him closer, sliding herself over his skin searching for every possible point of contact and almost screaming with sweet anguish as the sensations roared unchecked through her.

A tremendous effort bowed her body, striating her muscles into sharp definition, treating his weight as nothing, frightening him into awed acceptance of this new woman—a woman within whose being a brilliant light had suddenly come into being. Her body was no longer mere flesh and blood, but a newer and different medium into which had crept the unworldly, the super-conscious, the blossoming immortality of a plane where none is welcome save the favored and the initiated.

He ran a comb through his hair and returned it to his pockets. He was cool now, his old calm, assured self. "I didn't expect this, but I suppose I'm still human. I had it all made up in my mind to get you all ready, then leave. I couldn't do it."

Her eyes were somber and serious. "I wish you'd come back, Dan, but somehow I know you won't."

"No, I won't. You're a delightful pretty, Larry; but until you find a way to make yourself something more than that, you're going to come short. There are women who might not be as accomplished in making love as you, but they can do well enough at it and make a home for a man as well."

"You think I can't make a home for a man?"

"I rather think you could. A good one. You'd bear him fine children, too, and I think if you did you'd make an excellent mother. There's something fine about you and you're intelligent. Hidden away somewhere you've the capacity for a real lasting love."

"Thanks, Dan. I guess you ve been sweeter than I have any right to expect. I don't even hate you for telling the truth."

"That's a good sign. Remember that and you'll get along."

"You're not going to ask me what I'll do with Elsie?"

"No."

"Why?"

"Because you'll do what you'll do. I think you see it now for what it is." He grinned. "And you're not ruined for men, yet."

She smiled wanly. "That's nice to know."

"Chin up and all that," he said lightly. "Goodnight."

She lay stretched on the couch in a white wooly robe for a long time, floods of tears coming to her eyes. Elsie came in, her face white and her lips pressed together in a thin line. "Well … ?"

Larry looked at her and felt nothing. Never had she felt such a thoroughly negative attitude toward anyone who had been to her what Elsie had. "Well, what?"

The next morning Elsie left, bag and baggage without tears or recrimination, but her face was as set as a stone. When Elsie had gone, a vague restlessness seemed to surround her. She was appalled to find that there wasn't a single thing she could think of that might dispel the gloom, the nervous apprehensive fidgets.

She stood up, her lips taut and her nostrils flaring slightly, then without further ado she called the manager's office. "Mr. Aaron, I won't be needing my apartment after today. Will you send Ted and William up in two hours to take my things down, and please call the garage and tell them to give my car a complete servicing. Thank you."

She ran into the bedroom and began to pack feverishly, looking out at the dreary, grey day that seemed colder through the glass than it was in temperature.

CHAPTER THREE

LARRY had driven twenty-five hundred miles in four days and now she rode through pine scented air that held none of the northern chill. To her left she could catch glimpses of wide white beach and could see the sun glinting on tumbling waves.

Her rabid desire for speed had been satisfied and the escape impulse had died since she had escaped rather thoroughly from her old surroundings. She was conscious of an aching fatigue but it salved her nerves and produced a sense of relaxed well being. Birds flew across the road, jays as blue as an April sky, cardinals as red as dawn and tiny wrens as brown as the leaves they so resembled.

She pulled the big car off the road and stepped out. The sun was setting in a blaze of tropical splendor, turning the woods a weird vermilion hue, red spears of light filtering through the branches of the whispering pines.

She was dressed in scarlet culottes and a white shirt. Her black hair was confined by a turban of red silk. She stretched and wondered at the lack of traffic until she realized that she had taken the side road by preference. It was an excellent macadam road but it wound around a lot and there was little traffic except near towns.

She breathed deeply and arched her body in a huge relaxing stretch. She lit a cigarette and smoked for a while whereupon she began to feel the pangs of hunger. She smiled and tried to remember the last time she had really been hungry. She ate because she was a healthy human animal, but she rarely felt truly hungry. Now she could envision a thick succulent steak all pink in the middle and a rich brown on the outside, French fried potatoes, crispy brown on the outside and mealy white inside. Her mouth watered. With a leap that advertised her good spirits she struck the smooth leather upholstery and kicked the big car into action. "The very first likely looking spot," she said aloud, "I'm getting myself a real feed."

The first likely place she found was likelier than it seemed on first assessment. It was a log building that had been built with imagination and sat back in a veritable den of pines. The ground among the trees was smooth and padded heavily with pine needles, softening the ride of the car as she pulled up in front of the building.

She got out and sank into the soft carpet, stopped and sniffed appreciatively at the warm enticing odors that came from the back some place mingled with the pungent scent of the pines. A bubble of laughter came to her lips as she started into the building. With an exclamation of delight she walked toward a sleek Allard that caught her eye. It was black and cream and its upholstery was smoked elk. She caressed the flowing lines, then snatched her hand back as she realized that she might be marring the finish.

"Like her," came a voice.

She turned guiltily and saw a squarely built man of possibly thirty something. He had the appearance of being as solid as a block of oak, powerful but not large, his features, regular but not necessarily handsome. His face and hands followed out the square motif, the former tanned the color of hand-finished leather, the latter with long blunt fingers seemed to suggest tremendous power.

She smiled a trifle uncertainly. "I certainly do. It's an Allard, isn't it?"

"That's correct, Lincoln powered." He walked toward her and began to explain the points of the car, but she was now more interested in the way he filled the white cord suit and the fact that his tailor and his impeccable grooming had softened the blockiness of his build. He finished with the description and asked, "Have you eaten yet?"

"No ... and I'm starved. Is this a good place?"

"Excellent, thanks to Molly Moran's cooking. She can do things to meat. Joe might come in drunk and ruin your dinner, but that's a gamble you have to take. Will you join me?"

"Right now I'd gamble with the bull I can eat. Yes, I'll be glad to."

An hour later, she paused with a portion of steak halfway to her mouth. "Here we are chatting away like old friends and we haven't even met. I'm Laurent Dennison, Larry to my friends."

He smiled, the act lighting up his rather stern square face, and shoved a hand across the table. "I'm Jeffrey Wickware. The pleasure of this meeting is all mine."

"What makes you say that?"

He shrugged lightly. "My type comes a dime a dozen. You're a rarity."

"That car puts you in a class of your own," she said lightly.

"Sure. I bought mine. You were born with yours."

"Thanks for those kind words. I like the semi-flippant, semi-serious vein in which they were offered."

"The semi-flippancy was a maneuver to avoid sounding smitten."

"Are you?"

"No, but I could be if I were the sort of man who bent to his impulses."

In spite of herself she felt her pulses begin to race and her ears pounded to the heavy thrusts of blood. She shook herself mentally. This wouldn't do. For the past few days she had been free from that all powerful urge and this was no time to renew it.

"I should say," he murmured, "that you came from a very conventional background."

"I did. You have no idea how conventional, Jeff."

"And I'll bet that your conventional background has provided you with many a rough moment … that is, if you've really lived."

She caught her breath and her eyes lighted dangerously. "What do you mean by that?"

"Well …" His laugh was genuine. "I wasn't being subtle really, but you did spark on that one, didn't you?"

She felt ridiculous and flushed. "Go on. What did you mean?"

"Only that you seem to be a sophisticated woman if somewhat young. You're appallingly beautiful and you obviously have money. If you have never slept with a man I suggest with respect that you probably hold all records for resistance."

She felt the tenseness leave her and a strange feeling of smallness take its place. He was not being disrespectful or forward. His shrewdness was a little too well done for comfort. He was an intelligent man and was treating her like an intelligent woman, but she was reacting like any ordinary girl. The realization was not comforting.

"I'm sorry, Jeff. Maybe you can explain that to me."

"What?"

"You're right. My resistance hasn't been of the best, but automatically I resented you assuming the truth … although you didn't actually do that."

He nodded. "It's natural enough."

"So I've admitted I've taken some steps along the scarlet path … what does that do to the me you had begun to picture?"

His eyes narrowed somewhat. "To begin with, I dislike the term, 'scarlet path.' I've heard all my life about scarlet women, but for some reason men are never even a pale pink. I haven't the slightest right to expect more of you than I can produce myself, nor has any other man. They do, but that is a story all in itself. Not a pretty one I might add."

"You're the first man I ever heard admit that."

"Hurrah for me. I'm afraid I haven't a great deal of respect for my sex, taken as a whole."

"They're necessary," she said with a smile.

"I suppose so, but need they be so fatuous, so stupid, so utterly unrelievably dull? Have you ever attended a convention either business or political? Have you attended a business man's club?"

"No, to all of them."

"You should," he said with a shudder, "and you'd know what I mean."

"I thought they did good things."

"They do and to some measure mitigate the puerility of the joining impulse. I suppose I'm unreasonably opposed to any form of regimentation and thought control. Man's thoughts are controlled enough by the limitations of his intelligence, but to ask for more of it is the very epitome of stupidity."

She finished the last bite of steak and looked at him steadily. "Jeff, I like to hear you talk."

"Why?"

"Because your thoughts are so clear and you seem to have such perfect control over your speech. You say what you want to say. You haven't said I mean once."

He laughed softly. It had a feral sound that made a delicious shiver go over her. "Thank you." He ordered coffee for them and they lit cigarettes, drinking their coffee in silence. "What," he asked at length, "are you running from?"

She was not surprised. "Me, I suppose, and since this trip started, there seems to be a change for the better."

"A woman with money and too much time?"

"Something like that. My life didn't seem to have any direction."

"Has it now?"

"No, but I'm moving and that helps. Why is it one must have an objective?"

"In the sense you mean it, one doesn't."

"But one must have something to shoot at."

"Why not shoot at enjoying life? You'd be surprised how few people do."

She squashed her cigarette out irritably. "Jeff, I'm enjoying this too much. I shouldn't. I'll never see you again and now I'll feel a loss when I leave you?"

"That's the way fate maneuvers things. Maybe we'll have a common desire for a steak some day and meet at another place."

"Maybe, and the way I feel now, I'd like to maneuver fate."

He stood up. "Let it end on a good note. I may turn out to be a bastard of the highest order. If I stayed around you very long I should, I'm sure, begin to figure out ways to further your journey down the 'scarlet path.' "

She could smile this time and did. "And you know what? I might just cut short the figuring time by making you."

He paid the waiter chuckling. "I make awfully easy. Where are you going?"

"I don't have any idea. I'm just riding. I'll probably end up in Miami. Do you live in Florida?"

"Sometimes."

With that cryptic ending, they went outside; and after a brief farewell, the Allard swept grandly out of the drive onto the highway and disappeared. Larry pulled out after it, wondering what had kept them from exchanging addresses ... anything that would have helped toward a continuance of an acquaintance that in an hour's time had become more important than she was, at the moment, prepared to admit. She translated it into another facet of defeat and became unaccountably depressed. Depression coming as it did on the basis of four days of freedom and high spirits angered her and her foot went down.

CHAPTER FOUR

FOR fifteen minutes of straight excellent road she thundered the big car along at ninety-five miles an hour, but not once did she sight the sleek Allard. With a sigh she relaxed and allowed the car to slow to sixty-five and slid unobtrusively into a small town. There she refueled and bought several packs of cigarettes.

The attendant was a lazy boy of eighteen who lost his laziness with ludicrous abruptness when he had had a good look at her. He bustled about making suggestions, wiping and watching the automatic gas valve with an eagle eye. He even ran a grimy hand through his thick black wavy hair. He was a nice looking lad and she was amused at his hovering attention.

"Did you see an Allard come through ahead of me?" she asked.

"Sure, lady, that was Jeff Wickware. He has all the money there is."

"Where does he live?"

"God knows. Jeff just loafs around and lets his money make more money. He has a place in Miami, one in Fort Lauderdale and owns a few islands. Some says he has a mansion on all of 'em, but I got my doubts."

"He must be a character."

"You ain't got no idea. He *is* a character but he's a good guy. Uses awful big words though."

"He must be well educated."

"Some says he ain't ... hasn't any education past high school. Says he got it readin'."

"I guess he could at that. How much?"

"Lemme see. No oil, thirteen gallons of Extra. That'll be three seventy seven ... Oh, plus the cigarettes."

She signed a ten dollar travelers check and told him to keep the change. The lad flushed and grinned. "I wondered where the partyin' money was comin' from tonight. This'll do it. I sure thank you."

"Is there a good motor court in town?"

"Yes'm. Pringles. About a mile out of town."

She drove farther down the peninsula the next day, after a good nights sleep. As the day wore on, she began to feel better and by dusk she was feeling hungry again. Without realizing it, she was looking for the Allard and when she saw it, it seemed no more than natural that she should turn in and park beside it.

Jeff met her at the door and gave her his hand. "Welcome. I thought you'd never make it."

"I'm hungry," she said simply.

"I know and I have two of the most succulent red snapper steaks, broiled in butter, that you ever saw."

"Two of them?"

"Certainly, I felt sure you'd be here."

She said nothing but allowed him to lead her to the table, noticing that this place was better than the other one. It was paneled in blonde oak and the chairs and tables were of grey and red plastic. Potted plants stood about the walls and one whole side of the dining room was a tremendous indoor aquarium with every imaginable kind of tropical fish swimming lazily about.

They ate in comparative silence because Larry was noncommittal and hungry. Jeff ate steadily, but with a daintiness that spoke of careful and early table tutelage.

"I asked you once," he said softly, "what you were running from. I'll rephrase it. Where are you running to?"

"I don't know. I'm just moving."

"Do you have any intention of stopping anywhere?"

"Oh … possibly."

"And fall into the ways of the rich again. Get bored, then try to escape it by performing in the exact manner in which you found yourself at the cliff's edge?"

"I suppose so. Why?"

"Looks like you came a long way just for that."

She nodded. "Well, what else is there to do?"

He took out a cigarette, lit it and handed it to her. "What about a month or so on a beautiful island?"

"Sounds good. It'll give me time to think, sun and get fat. What's on your mind?"

"I have several and one is quite comfortable. I have a caretaker there and his family. They'd take care of you."

She smiled. "What's the trick?"

He smiled in return. "There're no strings. If I was purely on the make, I wouldn't go to such extremes."

"Then you admit that you might be on the make."

"Always," he said lightly. "Especially when there are women of your particular excellence about … assuming that such elegance is ever found in the plural."

"Where is this island?"

"Off the coast about seven miles. Just a quick run by speed boat."

"Why take me to the island where we'll be chaperoned? Why not to one where we could be marooned?"

He chuckled. "But for the baldness of that question, I'd say it was an oblique proposition."

She shook her head. "Not quite. I was just wondering."

"I won't be there. I just offered you the use of my island."

"That rings like a lead nickel. You mean my fair white body is in no danger of being in danger?"

"I didn't say that. It might possibly be, but in my event you'd have the last say. I'm no bluebeard."

She smiled and sat back. "That makes me feel better. What would I do on the island?"

"Just like you said. Sun, think, and get fat. You might even like to swim. It's a little cool yet, but some of the rugged ones are dipping regularly."

"You know, I might just take you up on that."

"Good. When can you leave?"

"I could leave right now."

"You could leave the island whenever the notion strikes you. I'll be over occasionally and probably throw a few parties."

"Goody ... and what'll you tell them about me ... ? Or do I keep out of sight?"

He laughed. "That's one of the privileges of money as you should know. You can act as eccentric as you please and everyone will think you're cute. I could have a dozen islands and as many mistresses and no one would think much about it."

"Do you have a mistress on every island?"

His eyes became opaque, but he smiled. "That's a state secret. Why do you ask?"

She shrugged. "I just wondered if I'd be another in a long line of mistresses ... and, of course, the thought that I would be, might make me balk."

"Spoken like a true virgin," he said with faint sarcasm.

She flushed. "Yes, I suppose it did sound pretty bad ... but what the hell. Lead on, Captain Kidd."

They found Johnny Elgin stalking about the deck of the *Snorter* taking a final swipe at the brass work. Immediately upon seeing him, Larry became intensely disinterested in brass work, slim gutted cabin cruisers, and other extraneous sights that abound about an upper crust boat dock.

Johnny Elgin was six feet tall, plus a few odd inches, burned to the color of the hull of the *Snorter*, the same sun having turned his massive pelt of dark brown hair almost white on top. The deeper it went the browner it became and in its present mussed state, seemed brindle. About his slim middle was a pair of faded khaki shorts that fit in such a manner that she knew he wore something else beneath them ... or else the fates had done him a horrible injustice. She shoved the thought from her mind and concentrated on the tremendous breadth of his shoulders and the smoothly rolling muscle that played about beneath the skin like live snakes.

"I'd say you were taken with Johnny," said Jeff quietly.

She smiled up at him. "And who wouldn't be? What a hunk of man!"

"Want him?"

"If I do, I think I can pull it off."

"You have a refreshing honesty, Larry," he said quietly. "That's why I like you."

She touched his hand. "Thanks, Jeff. I like you, too. Which boat is ours?"

"I don't have one here right now. We'll get Johnny to take us over."

"Is that his boat?"

"Yes. Johnny's an enigma. He doesn't talk much; so no one knows much about him."

"What does he do for a living?"

"It appears that he runs tourists around into odd bayous and bays and inlets such as are as thick as fleas in this area. He seems to know the Everglades like the palm of his hand. He's a top fishing guide, but I've seen him turn down good fishing parties because he didn't like the members ... so he said. He'll fight his weight in wildcats at the drop of a tattered hat. A very fascinating character."

"I'd say so, too. I feel it. Where does he stay?"

"On the boat. Some not-so-well-informed young man came lolloping along the dock one afternoon, feeling his oats, and leaped from the dock to Johnny's boat, probably scratched it a little. Johnny knocked him in the bay so cold he had to go get him out. Then the bravo goes and recruits some of his fellows and Johnny nearly killed them all with a spanner. Well, shall we go down and see if he likes us well enough to ferry us over?" They walked down the docks until opposite the *Snorter*. "Hey, Johnny," called Jeff.

The tall man raised up from his polishing and looked directly at Jeff without seeming to notice Larry. He nodded briefly in acknowledgment.

"How about running us over to Crane Cay?"

He bobbed his head slightly. "Sure."

To Larry, the man's eyes seemed volcanic. They smouldered under the permanently corrugated brow like coals ready to spring into flame. His chin was too powerful for the lax beautifully curved lips; but the Apolloesque neck, long and classic in line, was just right for the leonine head, with its unruly shock of heavy hair.

Jeff stepped lightly aboard with Larry's bags and put them down where a torpedo tube had been removed. "Johnny Elgin, may I present Laurent Dennison."

"How do you do," said Larry, her voice richly modulated.

Johnny nodded and pointed. "Better sit amidships. It's a little rough out tonight and I'm in a hurry."

"Got a date," asked Jeff jokingly.

"Far as I know you're only paying for ferry service," said Johnny shortly and touched a button that kicked the mighty engines into a roar that had a silken smoothness that belied the savage power they could unleash when fed.

Jeff shrugged and helped Larry into the cabin that was a dream in red and buff plastic, polished blond wood with contrasting mahogany, and colorful linoleum with a parquetry design. They took seats against the port bulkhead and Jeff nodded to her. "See what I mean?"

Larry was smouldering. "What's the matter with him? Can't he even be civil?"

"He's fine tonight. Better than usual."

"He's a waste," she said regretfully. "A total waste and he's too much of a man for that."

"What do you propose to do about it?"

"Nothing. I'm not taking anyone on as a liability. Let him find his level by himself."

The great engines thundered briefly in reverse, then the lean cruiser leaped away from the docking area with a burst of speed that made Larry clutch her seat. For five minutes they cruised slowly until they passed the head of a long breakwater, then the *Snorter* leaped again and the growl of the engines became a steady monotonous bellow. The boat smashed into smaller waves and seemed to leap bodily from larger swells, heeling over gracefully in answer to the powerful experienced hand on the wheel. In a matter of minutes, it seemed, the beat of the engines slowed then roared complainingly in reverse. There was a slight bump and the *Snorter* came to a stop.

"That was a fast run, Johnny," said Jeff as he led Larry on deck. "She's really ticking over good tonight."

"Tuned her up today," said the big man shortly. "That'll be five bucks."

Jeff paid him; and, as they stepped to the little floating dock, Larry turned and said very distinctly, "I'm glad to have met you, Mr. Elgin." She stood there, her jade green gabardine dress fitting with breathtaking exactitude, the low neck revealing the dark plunge between her breasts where they made their magic promise. Johnny took all this in with expressionless eyes, that were as steady as stones. For five long seconds he looked at her and gave her one of his stiff nods.

"And I think you're boat is wonderful. Do you use racing or utility props?"

At last she had startled him out of his rock-like reserve. He blinked and caught his breath. "Er ... I use the same props the Navy used, utility. You sound like you know boats."

"A little ..." She turned and walked away with Jeff toward the house that squatted on a rise ahead of them.

"What was that last little scene for," asked Jeff.

"I wanted to see if he was impregnable as he seemed."

"And you discovered that he wasn't?"

"Something like that. I'd say the boy's been badly hurt; and though I seem to sense that a woman is involved, that doesn't tell the whole story. I'm curious about him ... Jeff, what an odd house. Do you walk around on your hands and knees?"

He laughed. "That house is sunk eight feet into the ground and is made of reinforced concrete. I was caught in a hurricane here once in a frame house. The wind picked that house up board by board and blew it away from around me. Frankly, it scared the hell out of me and I built this one to stand anything but the island sinking. It has shafts of concrete imbedded thirty feet in the ground."

"It looks like a fortress." It did resemble a fortress but inside that impression was changed. The living room was a dream in cream and baby blue plaster with dark blue carpeting from wall to wall. Instead of corners, the room had been rounded out and in each half circle were comfortable couches built into the walls. One whole wall was devoted to book shelves, and big comfortable chairs in light blue leather were scattered about.

"Jeff … this is a … I don't know what to say. It's lovely." And so was the rest of the house. It had five bedrooms one of which was a sort of barracks with four three decker bunks made of natural finished beechwood. The walls were paneled in glossy coconut planks, the thready grain giving a very unusual effect.

The kitchen was nearly as large as the living room with every modern convenience. One wall even housed a tremendous freezer room. He opened the doors for her and let her see the ranks of frozen fowl, piles of cut and packaged steaks and tiers of frozen orange and pineapple juice. There were numerous other foods which she couldn't identify.

"Oh brother," she breathed. "What a retreat. There's enough food there for an army, Jeff."

"Sometimes I bring an army out. You should see them go through the food that Freyda cooks, too. You'll get fat for sure if you let her feed you like she'll want to. You'll find out tomorrow, but right now you probably want to get some sleep; so I'll take off. You can have the pick of bedrooms and the whole place is yours."

"Jeff, you know, you're pretty swell about all this."

He looked at her. "Just seeing you is reward enough. You're the most beautiful woman I've ever known."

She had a sudden foolish desire to cry. Her shiny black eyelashes grew moist. "Thanks an awful lot for saying that."

"You just needed to be told. You knew it already."

He was gone and the snarl of the boat dwindled in the distance leaving her alone in the stillness of the big house, relaxed, at perfect ease, and not in the least concerned about tomorrow.

She picked the bedroom done in rose and blue with a Hollywood bed and blond furniture. The faint hiss of air told her that the house was air-conditioned and the windows were high and closed.

She undressed and went into a bath that was tiled in rose and black with numerous mirrors that gave her any number of different angles from which to view herself. She tossed her hair until it became somewhat frowsy and tangled. She thrust out her lower lip, making a face at herself. She laughed a rich mellow laugh of complete freedom and began to examine herself and the bruises that Dan had left on her. She thought of that night and drew up and shivered, her stomach trembling with fresh desire. She took several deep breaths and stepped under an icy shower which served to relax her and quell somewhat the hot aching demand that threatened to interfere with her sleep. She went into the bedroom and turned out the light, stretching out on the bed, her limbs thrown carelessly in graceful ease.

Her mind started working again but soon sleep had confused Dan and Johnny to such an extent that it was Johnny who was taking her with bruising eagerness. The thought passed into a dream without a single missed sequence and so real was the smashing crescendo that she woke and lay in shuddering ecstasy for a long time, then fell into a deep slumber that admitted no dreams.

CHAPTER FIVE

THE next morning she had to stare at the ceiling with a frown for some time before she realized where she was. Then remembering, she smiled and stretched like a jungle cat; and with a flounce, landed on the red tile floor. She raced into the bath and took a cold shower, then punished her skin with a rough towel.

She dressed in scarlet silk shorts that came halfway down her thighs and a black T shirt that did wonderful things to the outlines of her breasts.

Breakfast was something she wanted now and she noticed the difference. She had a healthy hunger for food instead of a drink, the thought made laughter bubble deep within her.

She went into the living room, and hearing sounds in the kitchen, walked in. "Good morning," she said brightly.

Freyda turned and gave her a smile. "Good morning, Miss. You're Miss Dennison?"

"Yes ... and for goodness' sake Freyda, don't call me Miss Dennison. My friends call me Larry and I hope we're going to be great friends."

Freyda, a Nordic woman with corn tassel hair and pink cheeks like her daughter, eyed her closely. "If you don't mind me mentioning it, you aren't a bit like the other women Mr. Jeff has had here."

Larry smiled. "That sounds like a compliment."

"It is," said the woman seriously. "Why, some of 'em would lay in bed and wait for me to bring 'em breakfast. Lordy, how some of 'em would put on airs. Some of 'em wasn't much either. Real people don't act like that. Take you, you come in the kitchen with a "Good Mornin' " ready and start talkin' about bein' friends. That's the difference."

"Do you approve of Mr. Jeff's ways, Freyda?"

"His ways ain't my ways and that's all I can say. He's a good man and my children, Anna and Chris, is crazy about him. He spoils them rotten always givin' things to 'em and goodness knows me and Ole ain't worth what he pays us, but that's just his way. What he does is his own business and I don't never pry into it."

"That's a good attitude ... Freyda, have you cooked for your family yet?"

Freyda grinned. "No, ma'am. I didn't know what kind of queen you was goin' to pose as, so I come over here first thing."

"All right. Cook enough for them and let them eat here. I don't like to eat alone and there's no use of you cooking twice. I'll take a stroll along the beach and work up an appetite."

"Lordy," breathed Freyda. "I can see all over again that you ain't no trashy woman ... Honey, how come you're here? You don't look the type."

"The fact is, I'm just taking a vacation away from another kind of laziness, Freyda. Mr. Jeff didn't make any conditions when he offered me the use of the house."

Freyda shook her head. "Looks funny to me. What you want for breakfast?"

"You cook it and I'll eat it. Right now I feel like I could eat a barbecued horse. When I get back I'll feel like eating two."

She walked along the beach kicking in the sand with her beach sandals and feeling the bits of the fledgling sun nibbling at her skin. Later it would be hot, but now it was just right. She thought of Johnny and wondered what he was doing.

Johnny was talking to an old settler named Elford Barker, reputed to know everything about everyone for miles around.

Barker was talking, his whiskered chin bobbing occasionally as he gummed a load of Brown's Mule tobacco. "Questions," he snorted. "Looks t' me like ye got a passel o' questions to ast ever'time I see ye. I notice ye ain't answerin' none."

"I don't have to," said Johnny, his eyes darkening.

"Me neither," said Elf comfortably wiggling his toes in the sand. They sat in front of a shack that had been made of driftwood, Coca-Cola signs, trimmed gasoline tins and numerous other not so easily identifiable objects. He lived on a small island four miles from the mainland and had a powerboat in which he could be seen nosing about in unlikely places, sometimes guiding a carefully selected tourist. He did the selecting and said tourist might have to take, but would never be satisfied with, another guide.

Elf spat in the sand between his feet and sank back in his canvas chair. "Now I'll tell ye whut, bub. Tell me whut ye got on your mind ... all of it and I'll tell you what I can. I kinda got a hunch I know what's eatin' ye."

"You do? What?"

The old man's steel grey eyes glinted briefly. "Had you a gal onct, din't ye?"

Johnny's magnificent body tensed and ridges of muscles leaped into being across his back, shoulders and stomach. His face slowly went pale. He stopped with a strangled gulp and stood up. "You've said too much or too little, Elf."

"Control yerself," said Elf easily. "I know more'n ten whippersnappers like you."

"All right, tell me some of it."

"Ain't tellin' ye a suckin' word till ye tell me what ye got on yer mind. Go 'round makin' enemies, snappin' and snarlin' at people, turnin' down good tourist business cause ye don't like 'em ... Actin' like a plumb fool if ye asts me."

Johnny went limp and he flopped on the sand. "All right, you crusty old bastard. I'll tell you. My dad's name was Jackson Elgin ..."

"Know all o' that. Yer paw was the sharpest sawmill man in the state. Made a muckle o' money, then got shot one night at his boat wharf. Died next day 'thout comin' to. You come back from Korea that night and found out whoever killed yer paw took all three o' his fine boats ... and yer gal."

Little white dimples appeared on either side of Johnny's nose and his lips were bloodless. "How did you know all that?"

Elf shrugged. "Nemmine. Now go on and tell me somethin' I don't know."

Johnny straightened up. Little bullets of muscles appeared on either jaw. "Dad's murderer is free walking around and laughing probably. He got away with seventy-five thousand dollars worth of boats. And he got away with Mari." He stood up and began to pace up and down aimlessly. "I'm trying to find something and all I have to go on is a forty-five slug. That's the sum of the sheriff's efforts. He got the bullet that killed Dad and that's all."

"And you got somebody picked?" asked Elf.

"I sure have."

"Who?"

"I'm not talking about that. I'll tell you this much. That racer ... a man tried to buy it. Offered Dad fifty thousand for it and was refused."

"Unh hunh," grunted Elf. "Jeff Wickware."

Johnny was stung. "Now, how in the hell did you know that?"

"Simple, bub. Who was the man and what was the boat that always beat Jeff in them National Cup races? Yer paw ... and *Miss Torpedo, III.*" Simple that Jeff would try to buy it if he could."

Johnny's shoulders slumped. "All right, what's wrong with my pick."

"A boat like that racer o' yer paw's is like a old paintin', the value of it ain't in what it's got what can be broke down and sold. It was a good speed boat, faster'n anything within twenty-five horse-power. Jeff wanted the boat and he offered a lotta money for it. I don't see him shootin' nobody and stealin' a boat he couldn't race."

"He's been racing a boat that has actually showed more speed than Dad's ever did. How do I know that's not the boat? A paint job nad a few changes here and there would fix that."

"Maybe it is, but Jeff Wickware never killed nobody fer a boat. He mighta bought it offen the man what stole it."

Johnny tightened. "That's an idea, all right. I'll see what I can do from that end."

Elf spat again and this time he knocked the surprised mosquito hawk into a tail spin which it barely succeeded in correcting before it crashed. "Never heerd nothin' from Mari, did ye?"

Johnny went pale again. "Not a word, not a sign. None of her people have either. Let me ask you something. How do you know so much about me?"

"Knowed yer paw. Used to help him build boats. You was too young to remember. In them days we made *boats,* not none o' these here plywood cockle shells. How come ye took up with that Indian girl?"

"You're right on the verge of asking too much," flared Johnny.

"Sure, but me'n you's learned somethin' this mornin' and we ain't gonna git mad at one nuther."

Johnny's great shoulders slumped and his voice was a half whisper. "You're right and it feels better to talk. There just never was a woman like her. She was a dream in tan and jet and rose and she had fire that's burn you. She was wild and untamed, she was a hellcat from here to breakfast. She didn't have the usual reactions, and she had no education to speak of; yet she had read a lot and wasn't dumb. She could speak well and she could love. You always knew where you stood with her and she didn't know how to tell a lie. She had a body that, even thinking of it, makes me sweat. She was a savage and yet a sweeter girl never drew breath. The same person that killed my father probably took her, raped her, and chained her to a bed some place.

"Wimmen like that forget easy, bub. You was gone to the service. They have to have lovin'."

"Not her, Elf."

"Look here," snapped the old man. "Quit bein' a fool. *You* didn't stay ... true, is the word I think, and she didn't neither. Maybe she was raped, but a captive with any gumption don't make a man rape her ever' day. Comes a time when she gits tired fightin' and maybe she'll git to likin' it. Don't set around here and build yerself up fer no fall like that. 'Tain't smart."

Johnny's face twisted with pain but he nodded dumbly. "You're right, Elf."

"Sure I'm right and I'll tell ye sumpn else about them sorta wimmen. They're tough an', if she's still livin' an' got her health, she'll be all right if ye does find 'er."

Johnny suffered in silence for a while, scalding tears making bright trails on his cheeks.

"What do you know about a bird named Griff Griggs," he said at length.

"Nuthin' good. You got any ideas about him?"

"Some. Where does he get his money. He's got land, boats, and throws cash around like water."

"Lotsa people wonders about that."

"Sounds like you don't."

"Bub, I know more'n any ten people you ever seen."

"All right. What about Griff?"

"Weeel, I'll tell ye. The man takes off toward Cuba too often to suit me."

"You figure he picks up something?"

"I sure do, 'cept he don't go to Cuba."

"How do you know?"

"He ain't gone long enough … and he don't never go on clear days."

"Think he's running drugs?"

"Mebbe … booze is gittin' profitable again since all the taxes got put on."

"Where'd he come from?"

"God a'mighty knows. He showed up one day with a string o' boats."

Johnny flinched. "I think I'll have a chat with Mr. Griggs."

"Better watch him. He's a mean hombre."

"Me too," gritted Johnny, his breath whistling through his nose.

"How come you so slow pickin' on him," asked Elf, closing one eye.

"Oh … I don't know. No one seems to know a lot about him, and I couldn't get my mind off Jeff Wickware."

"Jeff might help, but he ain't killed nobody. Jes' ast him where he got the *Jetfish*."

"And what if he won't tell me."

"That's your hoss, bub. You'll ride him one way or t'other."

Johnny discovered that finding Jeff Wickware was something of a chore and finally he turned the *Snorter* toward Crane Cay and opened the throttle wide. The eager craft leaped and sculled across the sound like a gull taking off. He whirled it up to the dock and gunned it in reverse, then killed the engines and let it drift into the wharf where it touched gently.

After a bountiful breakfast which she ate with a gusto, making Freyda's eyes glisten with pleasure, Larry sat back with a cup of fragrant coffee, her third and enjoyed the Neilsons. Ole was a huge, slow talking Scandinavian with kindly blue eyes and a ready grin. Chris was an underdeveloped counterpart of his father, with fair youthful skin, deep serious eyes and a frame that would one day be big boned and powerful. Even now he was nearing six feet and his shoulders were growing broad. Anna was a chatterbox and seemed always at good natured war with her brother. Larry was smitten by the aura of passionate animal attraction that the big girl seemed to exude like a rare perfume. She was not in a spot where any coquettishness would show and somehow Larry doubted that the girl was so inclined. She didn't need to be. Dressed as she was in white shorts and a shirt, filled to the bursting point with top grade flesh she had no need of coquetry. She'd cause a stampede just by being present. She fidgeted about a great deal; and when she'd move, the act would make her breasts nod and bounce inside the shirt raking the cloth with tips that seemed to stay erect. After breakfast they went their various ways and Larry went to her room to dress for swimming, exploring, or sunning.

She met Anna outside and asked her to act as guide.

"How big is the island," Larry asked Anna as they walked toward the northern tip.

"One and a half wide by two long. It's small. See all the coconut trees? Mr. Jeff planted them. There was nothing but the pines at one time and a few scrubs."

"There's plenty of them," said Larry.

"There's a pool up the hill there too." She pointed up the gentle rise where the pines sawed the horizon jaggedly. "When it rains it stays full. It's full now and we go there to wash off the sea water when we swim."

"Is the water too cold for you?" asked Larry.

"Jeepers no. Chris and I swim the year round."

"Doesn't it get lonesome here?"

"It wouldn't if there were some men over here."

"You like men?"

"Love 'em. Larry, I wish I was sophisticated like you and knew things."

"Things like what, dear?"

"Like what men do ... Oh goodness, maybe I'm insulting you."

Larry laughed merrily. "Oh, no, you haven't offended me."

Anna hugged the tree shiveringly. "I love this island, but I do wish it had more men on it. Oh, I almost forgot. There is one coming in a day or so."

"Who?"

"I don't know him. Pop says he's just a boy, but one of the best boat repairmen around. Pop got Mr. Jeff to stake him to a couple of old cruisers and the boy is coming to put them in shape. Then Pop and Chris will take tourists and fishermen out for sailfish and marlin."

Larry could see the anticipatory gleam in the girl's eyes and thrilled vicariously. Anna was so bursting with healthy vitality that she could scarcely contain herself. She whirled about and sat down, displaying her legs proudly.

"Anna, your legs are beautiful," said Larry in honest admiration.

Anna tossed her thick mane of golden hair and extended the smooth white column before her, pointing the foot straight out. It was not a small leg, but it was so shapely, so incredibly well turned, so crammed with solid flesh, so marble smooth that Larry swallowed involuntarily. On the surface a faint dusting of golden hair as fine as spiderweb glinted in the rays of the sun.

"You like them?" she asked with a touch of shyness.

"They're simply lovely and so long and wonderfully constructed. You think you'll like the man who is to repair the boats?"

Anna giggled. "Unless he's dirty and posolutely *ugly* I'll like him. Do you reckon he'll like me?"

Larry chuckled. "Unless he is posolutely made of stone he will."

"Let's take a swim, Larry," said Anna, getting to her feet with a fluid bounce. "I'm so full of myself I don't know what to do."

"I didn't bring a suit," said Larry, dubiously.

"We'll go to the freshwater pool. It's all surrounded by brush and trees. We don't need suits. I hate 'em anyhow."

Fifteen minutes later, they stood on the narrow graveled bar that made a half circle around the pool that had been gouged out by the rain. The pool was deep and clear, shaded, cold, and inviting. They stood on the gravel, one a goddess of the North, a Norse siren carven plentiously from white voluptuous materials crowned with a cataract of silken gold.

The other was a goddess from the South. Her crown was as black as night, falling to her shoulders in glistening waves, her skin faintly olive, touched with creamy ivory gold. She was slimmer in body and cast in a more classic mold. Both had trim waists and ankles and both were rich and firm in breasts, the four high lifted mounds of lush beauty tipped in pink, excited into sharp rosebud attention by the cool atmosphere.

"You're beautiful, Larry," said Anna raptly, earnestly.

"You make me feel old and baggy," scoffed Larry as she whirled and slid expertly into the water.

CHAPTER SIX

JOHNNY, feeling that he had made a trip for nothing, skirted the house and looked for Jeff at a distance. He'd prefer to see without being seen. Jeff might be on the other side of the island so he decided to walk across.

Johnny cut through the thick woods that rode the high ground back of the house. Long a man of nature, native caution and habit made him skirt obstacles rather than crash through them so he came quietly within earshot of the pool. Hearing laughter, he crept to the fringe of bushes surrounding it and peeped over. His muscles flexed and tightened in one startled reaction. Below him in the crystal clear waters, two mermaids frisked like sportive dolphins. One, white, pink and gold, firm and plenteously fleshed and the other a dark-haired naiad, long and deliciously curved, standing now knee deep in the water, her skin jeweled with opalescent globules of water, stray rays of the sun sparkling on her divine surface, making a brooch of unearthly beauty. The tableau made Johnny's heart smash against his ribs with alarming force. For a while he watched as Larry would slip like a softly cast javelin into the water with hardly a ripple while Anna would slide her ravishing body slowly through the water in twisting undulations with the ease of a slothful porpoise, then they'd repeat or change places. Johnny drew quietly away and, once in the clear, almost ran from the spot, wiping his face with a trembling hand.

It was a useless venture this search for Jeff, so he made his way back to the docks, his mind racing furiously and his heart still pounding from the capsule of loveliness he had left in that watery caché on the far side of the hill.

A boat raced across the little bay toward the docks.

Jeff stepped lightly ashore and waved. "Hi, Johnny."

The other didn't reply, but walked close to the smaller man. "I want to talk with you, Jeff."

"Certainly ..." He turned to the boatman. "That's all right, Ed. I won't be going back with you now. Come back at eight." He spoke to the other passenger that had come ashore with him. "You go on to the house, Jesse. You'll find Ole around some place. Leave your tools here and he'll take you around the point in the dinghy. That'll be better than carrying them."

Jesse, a wonderfully slim youth with a thick shock of brown curly hair and shoulders that seemed too big for the rest of him, nodded and walked away.

"Now, Johnny, what's on your mind?"

"Where did you get the *Jetfish?*"

Jeff smiled tightly. "I recall yesterday I asked you a question, a kidding harmless question, and you reminded me that I had paid for a ferry trip and that was all. What are you paying for?" Jeff's jaw grew as hard as iron. "Your question was impertinent and none of your business ..."

"And the one you asked is important?"

Jeff sighed. He was about as irritated as he ever allowed himself to become. "What makes you think you can just walk the hell over everyone, be uncivil and cantankerous, then make any demand you want and have it granted?"

"I'm asking you a civil question and I want an answer."

"And you don't get it."

"I'm asking again, Jeff."

"The answer is the same." There was no time to block or duck the devastating left hook and Jeff took it on the side of the head, spun around three times and went into the water. He came up, swam to the dock and pulled himself up where he shook his head several times, a crooked little grin twisting his square face.

"I am forced to believe you're serious, Johnny."

"A late, but correct assumption," said Johnny, waiting.

Jeff nodded, got slowly to his feet. "So I see, but I don't like your methods." A hand flashed out and the sharp edge of it cracked into the jaw, neck, ear area. Johnny went totally blind for a split second, his head roaring with pain, but in that space another iron hard hand struck his Adam's apple and another buried itself wrist deep in his relaxed midsection. He doubled up with pain and as he did an axe seemed to explode against the base of his skull and he slid into a soft puffy cloud of nothingness.

When he came to, he was seated on the dock with his back against a piling while Jeff sat a few feet away quietly smoking a cigarette.

"Now let's go at this thing like a couple of intelligent humans," he said gently.

Johnny, with the mad knocked out of him, for the moment, was overcome by a desire to laugh. He managed a grin and nodded. "All right. I forgot that you had a degree from the Yamoshida school of Judo. I'm a little slow, too."

Jeff shrugged. "An accident I assure you. I was roughed up in Tokyo by a thug, so I managed to get Yamoshida to teach me a few tricks. I dislike being roughed up."

"So I see. Now in all seriousness, where did you get the *Jetfish?*"

"Suppose you tell me what's eating you and I'll consider your questions. I rather suspect you have more than one."

Johnny sighed and nodded. "I have a lot of them. I'm surprised that you don't know what I want to know."

Jeff's brow knitted in thought. "You're a strange one, Johnny, and since you've been around, no one seems to have learned much about you. I'm not a hard man and I'd like to be your friend. I've tried, but you didn't seem to want to go along. Now suppose you tell me what's on your mind and maybe I can help. I'd like to. What just happened was, I suppose, necessary, but I think that since we're both grown men we can forget that."

"Sure …" He shook his head. "I'm not right in the head, Jeff. I guess I've been going about this all wrong. You know my last name, don't you … ?"

Jeff snapped erect with a start. "Elgin … boat …" He stood up with a single smooth effort. "Holy Joseph … You're not Jackson Elgin's son?"

"That's right. Now do you know?"

Jeff nodded slowly. "I see a lot now. You knew I wanted *Miss Torpedo, III* and …" He grinned crookedly. "I thought I had camouflaged her better than that. And I juiced her up, too. Added fifteen horsepower to the power plant and now she'll break any mark your dad ever made. He was more intent on hull and prop design than anything else. She's the sweetest boat I ever owned."

"Where did you get her?"

"I bought her from Griff Griggs."

"Where did he get her?"

"Well, Griff's a sort of horse trader in boats, you know. He said he got her in a trade."

Johnny stood up. "So here's where we are. Either Griggs murdered Dad and stole the boat with the others, or he traded with the man who did. I'm going to get him, Jeff, hear me?"

Jeff reached out a powerful hand and took Johnny's. "I hope you do and let me know if I can help. I bought the boat, Johnny, because I wanted it worse than anything. I knew it was your dad's boat once. I knew that he had been murdered, but I didn't know the boats had been stolen. That didn't get into the papers."

"Two cruisers also disappeared. Did Griggs offer you any cruisers?"

"No, he didn't offer me any. You know, I feel guilty about this. I thought a great deal of your father and it is certain that he was the absolute tops in boat designing. I didn't think about the racer having any connection with his death … and yet dammit, I should have." He shrugged. "Why rail about it? I wanted that boat the worst way; and even if I had thought about it, I doubt that I could have resisted buying it."

"You're honest about it at any rate," said Johnny with a grim smile. "I'll be shoving. I have a date with Griff."

"Be careful," said Jeff warningly. "That mug impresses me as being a poisonous snake. Treat him like one."

Johnny turned to go but stopped and came back. "Thanks a lot, Jeff. I guess I've been wrong about a lot of things."

The other flipped a depreciatory hand. "Now that I know, I can't say I blame you. Good hunting."

It was late afternoon when Johnny Elgin sighted the sprawled elegance of Griggs camp as it sat on the high mound. He spun the wheel in his hands and minutes later had tied up alongside several cruisers and various other craft that tugged sleepily at their painters.

He stepped on the dock and started up the steps leading to the well-kept lawn in front of the house. When the gate came in sight he noticed that a man now leaned negligently against it with a short dead cigar in his mouth.

"Lookin' for someone," said the man in a hard unpleasant voice.

"Yeah," rasped Johnny just as hard, never breaking his stride. "I'm looking for Griff Griggs."

"He ain't here," said the man, but he was smart enough to stand away from the gate because Johnny was obviously coming through.

"I said he ain't here," persisted the man standing back from the gate, but still blocking the ornate brick path.

"I'll see for myself," said Johnny, still walking. The other was thick at the shoulder and stomach, but he didn't appear sick or weak. He put out his hand and brought Johnny to an abrupt stop. "Don't go a step farther, chum."

"Get out of the way."

"Better take it back to your boat."

"You'd better stand aside and quick."

"I'm planted, chum."

"Okay." The left was a short one but it had been thought out and behind it was the full power of Johnny's tremendous shoulders. It cracked sharply on the fellow's chin and Johnny stepped over the prone body and walked on to the house seeing for the first time the several men on the wide verandah.

A big thick chested man got up and opened the door. He was middle aged but his hair was still stiff and black although his face and stomach spoke of too much whiskey and rich food.

"Come in," he said jovially, "since you can't be turned around."

"I don't like to be turned around," said Johnny. "You Griggs?"

"Yeah, that's me. What can I do for you?"

"I'm John Elgin."

"Sure you are," agreed Griggs heartily. "Have a chair."

He took one and hesitated, having been taken aback somewhat by Griggs reply. He wasn't quite sure what he had expected, but this blandness wasn't it.

"I'd like to ask you some questions."

"Shoot."

"I'd like to know about that racer you sold Jeff Wickware."

Griggs screwed a long cigarette into a longer holder. "Freeman, go help Tim. Take him around back and sluice some water over his head. He don't look happy." Freeman, slender, but hard, got up and with a blank look at Johnny went out to Tim who was trying to get up but not too successfully.

"Now, what was that question … ? Oh, about that racer. Mighty nice boat. Fast and stout. Jeff's got back what he paid for it in prize money."

"Where'd you get it?"

Griggs looked him over genially. "What you want to know for, son?"

"Because my father was killed trying to keep it from being stolen."

There were twin intakes of breath, a chair scraped a little and a dead silence settled, making Tim's curses from the back of the house easily audible.

Johnny's heart began to sing. They hadn't connected him with the murder victim and had been startled when they did.

"You do ask questions, don't you," said Griggs softly, "but I'll answer 'em. I bought the boat off a guy."

"What guy?"

Griggs shrugged. "How should I know? I buy boats all the time. Sell 'em too."

"You don't remember who it was?"

"Clear forgot … complete."

Griggs stood up, his easy friendly manner gone, his eyes as hard as glass. "Sorry I can't help you any, Elgin. Drop around again sometimes."

"I will," said Johnny, standing. "Maybe you'll let me go out some rainy day when you point for Cuba."

Griggs stiffened and his face froze into hard blank lines. "Sure," he said softly, "any time at all. Make it soon, will you?"

CHAPTER SEVEN

JOHNNY ELGIN, foaming with rage and chagrin headed toward Crane Cay without knowing where he was going. He steered mechanically and felt a certain exultation grip him through the fires of his rage as the fleet craft soared along splitting crests and sending clouds of spray sheeting out from her sharp bow.

He didn't pull into the bay, but skirted the northern tip and throttled back to creep at slow speed southward, realizing as he did why he had headed for Crane Cay. Subconsciously he had hoped to see Larry again; and, being a brutally honest man especially with himself, his reaction was not one of resentment but of excited amusement ... and there she was standing out on a thin sand spit, the wind moulding her soft white dress to her lush body with heart stopping effect.

He nosed carefully in and crept close to shore, his big body tense and tuned to catch the first grate of the sand on the bottom. It came and he throttled back furiously freeing the bow, then he cut his engines and walked on deck. "You look lonesome," he called.

To Larry he looked like a god, stripped to the thin tight fitting trunks, his tanned body gleaming in the white light of lunar illumination. She went weak and giddy, her mouth drying suddenly and her blood rocketing in savage thrusts through her veins.

"I *am* lonesome," she said with a wave of her hand, "but I'm no better off now. I can't swim that far in these clothes."

"Take 'em off," he said with a grin, the first she had seen and she was struck with the relief it afforded his rather stern face.

"That'll be the day. I'd freeze to death in wet clothes."

"Well, you force my hand. I'll come get you in the dinghy." He went below and came back with a rubber dinghy and an air bottle. He inflated the frail craft and threw it, leaping into the water after it and climbing agilely aboard. He unhooked a short aluminum paddle and soon was holding the nose of the dinghy to the sand spit so she could clamber aboard.

"When I let you out I'll take you around to the dock," he said.

"You say that as though it'll be next year."

He grinned and dug the paddle deep, sending his shoulders into knotted bumps as the muscles slid smoothly and tensed beneath his dark hide. "You have some place to go?"

She held her arms up to the skies and threw her head back, the effect of the pose on her breasts making him miss a stroke and nearly fall overboard.

"No place to go and all my life to get there."

They were at the *Snorter* and Johnny stood, gathered her in his arms and boosted her easily to the rail where she caught hold and clambered aboard, her skin growing hot and prickly as she realized that she must have few secrets from him now. He gave no sign that he had looked and, catching the painter in his teeth, leaped aboard and pulled the dinghy after him.

He dropped anchor to stop the craft from drifting and showed her below.

"How would a drink strike you?"

"Fine," she said trying to quell the trembling in her stomach. "What's come over you all of a sudden. You were a regular bear the last time I saw you."

"I've had my troubles," he said easily, opening a built-in bar and pouring. "I'm a rye drinker. What'll you have?"

"I'll drink with you. I'm no alcohol epicurean. Don't a lot of people have troubles?"

"I suppose so, but I'm beginning to see a light, and although I ran into a dead-end today I'll eventually find out something and then ... Oh *brother.* A guy I know will be in trouble."

He came and sat beside her. They drank and talked. Larry's attention was divided between listening, savoring his nearness—the symmetrical bulk of him, the faint scent of strong, clean man with its admixture of whiskey and tobacco, and willing her clamoring body into a semblance of behavior.

She told him such of her past as she deemed fitting and listened to some of his stories of the war in Korea. This consumed several drinks and soon they were both feeling unworldly and exultant.

"God, but you're beautiful," he said after a brief silence.

"Thanks," she said with a faint smile. "I was beginning to wonder if I weren't hideous."

"That's spoken like a woman ... but you knew."

"A woman never knows when she meets a new man. She's off on a new adventure and must be told each time. She never tires of it."

He sat back, his mouth grim. "And every time I think of a woman, a beautiful woman ... Nope ... not tonight. I feel too good, and you're too beautiful to harbor morbid thoughts."

She knew he had been about to tell her about *the* woman; and, though she was curious, she, too, didn't care to have another woman intrude on their little world.

"Want to take a ride?" he asked.

"Where?"

"About ten miles southeast there's a little island. Not much bigger than a football field, but sort of cute. I can run the nose of the *Snorter* on the sand there because deep water goes right up to the beach. It has a few trees and a lot of brush. Very very private."

"Lead me to it. I have always wanted an island all my own."

He upped the anchor and soon the *Snorter* was slicing through waves, riding out swells. It was not a long run and Johnny soon had the sharp prow of the craft hanging over the narrow beach, holding her steady at slow throttle while Larry, a huge blanket in her arms, leaped over the bow and fell sprawling on the beach.

He roared with laughter, killed the engines and followed her with a rope which he strung out and tied to a gnarled root protruding from the sand.

She picked herself up and slapped the sand from her dress. "I'll get you for that laugh," she promised.

He laughed again and began to pick up driftwood and broken branches. "Come in here," he called. "I'm going to build a fire and we don't want to attract any curious people that might be joyriding."

He built a roaring fire in a sandy little clearing, shut off from the ocean by a dense growth of brush, and spread a blanket some distance away. She sat on it and drew her legs up, primly pulling her skirt over her knees.

"You accepted this venture without a question," he said flinging himself beside her, propping up on one muscular arm. "Suppose I'm a hellion."

She laughed. "Is that bad?"

"Most women would pretend it is."

"I'm not most women and I'm a little brutal, I'm so forthright. Men have some quaint idea that women fear and resist all attempts on their virtue. A great deal of that attitude is tactics."

He smiled slowly, his eyes questioning. "You are pretty forthright. Suppose I said I've wanted to kiss you since I spied on you and Anna in the pool yesterday?"

"You utter dog … Well, I'd say time's awastin'."

He shook his head. "That's being too forthright. It's not so. Not you at any rate."

"You think there's a catch?"

"I surely do."

She leaned over and kissed him full on the mouth, clutching him about the neck and burying her mouth in his, her lips parting and her tongue sending an upsurge of shattering reaction through his body.

When she released him he was not quite conscious. "Now," he breathed, "you not only made a lie of me, you did it the only way you could have."

"Now will you behave?"

He shook his head. "I might have until you did that. Horses couldn't hold me now."

She fell into his arms, her body slowly getting the upper hand of her will. Her lips were parted and her eyes glassy with desire. "You talk too damn much, Johnny Elgin."

Thunderstruck, he looked at her for a few seconds, letting the fire play redly over her ivory skin, glinting on her glossy hair that was now disordered and flooding over his arm.

He kissed her and felt the rippling response that sent little battalions of rigors flicking through her body in waves. Her nostrils snared hungrily for air and he could feel the prod of her hard breasts against his naked chest.

His hands wandered gently over her back and flank on to the rapturous curve of her hip and thigh, retracing itself and stopping at her waist and tugging her in gently. She responded and forced herself against him, her throat working with ecstatic sounds that were impossible to voice.

For a long time they drank from each other's lips until Larry thought she would go mad, awaiting the reward for the lashing demands of her body. She was conscious of a peculiar hypersensitivity that made her skin contract and react to the slightest stimulation. Her panties, cutting into her legs where the elastic drew it tight, seemed to be twin belts of flame and the tips of her breasts seemed to sear themselves against his chest.

"Johnny," she whispered fiercely, "Johnny, I want you so ... all of you. I need you ... now."

"I need you," he replied gutturally, "... and now."

With a spring she leaped out of his arms and stood for a moment, every muscle trembling, looking down at his long, lithe body aripple with conditioned sinews, young, healthy, and clean. Slowly, she unbuttoned the dress down the front, watching the slight muscular evidence of his reaction as it finally slid in a heap at her feet.

"Beautiful," he muttered sitting up. "Beautiful and all fire and eagerness. You burn me even at this distance."

"You started burning me farther than this," she said as she unhooked her brassiere but stood holding it in place for a moment.

"Take it off," he hissed frantically.

She still held on, feeling very naked and vulnerable in her loosened bra, half slip and frothy gestures of briefs. Her stomach heaved jerkily as her breath staggered and grew ragged. He leaped and caught her around the waist, pulling her to him. The confinement disappeared and the impact of his lips was like a branding iron. She sobbed out a cry and dug her nails into his neck, sliding them upward to clutch his shaggy hair and forced his head into the swelling ivory mounds of pink tipped wonder.

His hands slid slowly under her slip, accelerating a cry that seemed to lay in wait in her throat. Inch by inch they crept upward sending her body into a series of convulsive seizures. He held her with sure strength, but she writhed trying to facilitate the reaching of his objective, a wall of flame eating at her vitals demanding to be quenched or consumed. Her lips roved beggingly over his face, trying to hold the voice of the precariously dammed passion that threatened momentarily to blast its way to release. The hands stopped and lifted her slightly and she felt a cooler sensation and heard the sibilant swish of her briefs as they landed on the blanket.

"Johnny, don't make me wait … Oh, Johnny … … Johnny." She wept and writhed losing her grip on the situation, so avid and hungry was her need.

With main strength she pulled him over, to her. Larry opened her mouth, held it so for a moment, then relaxed a little, her arms crushing him closer into the embrace while nature searched blindly and blindly discovered, wrenching from him a groan of unutterable joy and from her lips the immortal song of victory.

Higher and higher mounted the ascent into that ineffable stratosphere where the keen searing heat of love is highest, rhythm being surplanted by mad tyrannical haste, where mountain waters, long quiescent, tumble down steep rocky gulches to inundate them in a sweeping torrent of remission.

The fire died and the wind cold on their skin woke them from their deep, dreamless sleep.

He sat up and tried to collect his scattered faculties.

Her lips came sleepily to his. "Darling, hold me tight ... tight ... Ahhh." A sob came from her throat and she held to him like a drowning woman.

"We'd better take a dip now," he said gently. "It's getting late."

She nodded, and with a final convulsive contraction of her arms, she released him. They both stood up and walked into the chill waters, played about for a while, then he boosted her to the deck essaying an intimacy that made her lose her grip and fall back on him.

"You pick the worst times," she whispered. "I might have hurt us."

He laughed and boosted her up again and this time she straightened up on deck.

"I'll bring the clothes," he said, "and that'll keep you from having to wash the sand from your feet."

He returned with their clothes and found her massaging her stomach and hips with a look of distaste in her eyes. "I'm all sticky from that salt bath," she complained.

"I'll fix that." He disappeared and came back bearing a bucket of water. "Stand still and I'll sluice you down."

She stood straight, screamed when the water touched her skin. He continued to douse her, having to chase her about the deck in order to do so.

"You *dog ... ice* water," she chattered.

"Close up your pores," he said choking with laughter.

"I want them open," she said as she accepted a big rough towel and began to scrub her body.

When she finished she noticed that he was staring at her, his eyes having lost their mirthful gleam.

"Johnny ... what ... ?"

"Larry, come here."

She went to him wonderingly; but when her body melted to his, she wondered no longer, the lashing spurt of blood, heating her into trembling, supplicating reaction in an instant.

He bore her backward to the deck where the blanket had been tossed, his muscles ridging against her stomach, a hard thigh demanding entry. A weak sob welled in her throat.

Movement met movement, movement that soon forgot fatigue, seeking frantically for that which lay at the end of the path and at last finding it in a rippling blaze of passion that surpassed anything she had ever known, leaving her limp and only partly conscious.

When at last they moved apart, the moon was half a coin on the western horizon and the light that surrounded them was weird and pallid.

CHAPTER EIGHT

WHEN Johnny pulled into his home dock the sun was pinking the horizon a delicate shade and tendrils of thin mist writhed like pale ghosts off the surface of the water.

He secured the craft to the dock and with a prodigious yawn went below and took a quick shower. He came out of the tiny cubicle scrubbing his body vigorously and almost went to his bunk without noticing the stocky individual sitting in the tiny salon with a huge cigar clenched belligerently between his teeth. He frowned and stepped through the doorway twisting the towel about his middle like a *lava-lava*. He knew the man slightly and liked him a great deal less. He was a local biggie in political circles and loved his reputation immensely.

"What do you want?" asked Johnny as rudely as he knew how.

"Hi, Johnny," said Erico with a wave of his hand showing off a diamond that looked fresh out of an ice tray. "Just a sociable visit. Don't you like company?"

"Sometimes ... when it bathes regularly."

Erico's grin showed the effort it had cost. He was a man of certain tender sensibilities, if equally possessed of other senses that were apparently armor plated. His personal pride was a thing of considerable ferocity and Johnny had wounded it mortally.

"Pretty free with the tongue, ain't you, Johnny?"

"Not any freer than you are with my boat. Get the hell off it before I chunk you in the drink."

Erico's dark greasy face grew darker. "I come here to tell you something and I was all ready to make it as light as I could but you fed the hand that bit you ... I mean bit ..."

"I know what you mean. You mean Griff Griggs sent you. All right, what did he tell you to tell me ... since you've turned into a glorified messenger boy?"

Erico turned purple and resisted an impulse to murder. "Better get your head straight on that, boy," he growled, controlling his voice with a mighty effort. "I'm the one what gives orders around here ..."

"I see. Then maybe you're the guy to ask about those wet weather voyages Griff goes on. I'm interested."

Erico came smoothly to his feet. "Why are you interested, Johnny?"

"That's *my* business ... what's yours, dope smuggling?"

Erico lost his purple tinge with disconcerting suddenness. "What's it to you?"

"Nothing to me. I just happened to ask Griff a question ... not interested really and look what happens? All of a sudden a politician is interested ... and touchy. Back at you ... How come?"

Erico flexed his shoulders and his face became calmer. He even uttered a short mirthless chuckle. "You like it here, Johnny?"

"I like it."

"All right. You better stick to boats. If I took the notion you might not like it too much."

Johnny's eyes went stony hard. He stepped forward and slid out a left that popped sharply on Erico's fat chin and sent him reeling into a bulkhead, clawing at his left shoulder, but Johnny was on him like a tiger. Instead of trying to arrest the hand going after the gun he slammed a terrific right and left low in the man's stomach, sending him folding over with a gusty bleat. Then Johnny smashed a hard knee squarely into Erico's face.

He grabbed him around his fat middle and carried him on deck, Erico's snubnosed .45 in his left hand. He hurled him carelessly onto the dock and stood waiting while three henchmen detached themselves from the lightening shadows of a boat house and dashed forward. They stopped, stared at their fallen idol, one of them making a sudden motion toward his shoulder only to be stopped by the dead eye of the gun in Johnny's hand.

"Take that bag of crap and get going with him," grated Johnny, "and if I see any of you again it had better be at a distance."

They started away with Erico's limp body and Johnny turned to go below again.

"Hey there, Johnny."

He turned to see the lank figure of Sheriff Lane slouching in his direction.

"Mind if I have a word with you?"

"No. Come on aboard. I got to get into some clothes."

Clad in fresh shorts, Johnny flopped into a deck chair and raised his legs over the arm of the chair. "What's on your mind, Cal."

The sheriff was a man so gaunt that he seemed about to fall apart with a slouching walk that intensified the impression. His face was deceptively mild as were his pale blue eyes. A ragged moustache with drooping points made his face appear doleful and bloodhound-like.

"I seen Erico go aboard your boat, so I hung around. Think it's smart to head into him?"

"This is my boat, Cal. I don't like a threat anytime. On my boat it goes double."

"Ummm. Threaten you, did he?"

"He did."

"About what?"

"You're full of questions, Cal."

Lane fashioned a cigarette of King Bee and brown paper, glued it to his lower lip and squinted mildly at the younger man. "I'm the sheriff, son," he said gently. "I'm on your side. I'd like to stay on it."

"Lookin' for your dad's murderer, I'd hazard."

"Right and the first lead I get runs me afoul of Erico Pucci."

"That's what I'm interested in. Me'n you're on the same side like I said."

Johnny was suddenly aware, in a manner that escaped detection, that here was a man whom most people, including himself, misunderstood. Cal Lane was definitely not a fool.

"Maybe we are, Cal ... at that."

"Sure we is."

"You had your eyes on Griff Griggs?"

"I got my eye on ever'body. Don't seem necessary to let 'em know it, somehow. Lotsa folks, Johnny, like to think I'm sorta thick between the ears. Well, that's all right, too, but one day ..." He seemed to grow drowsy in his chair.

His eyes opened again and looked directly at Johnny. They weren't mild any more. "You ain't very communicative."

"What do you want to know? You know why I'm here."

He tapped ashes carefully into the cuff of his drab trousers and nodded. "Maybe we'd better work together if you can see your way clear. Might be better in the long run."

"All right. Fire away."

"First I'll tell you a few things I know. Maybe it'll help you. I know 'em, but I can't prove 'em. Griff goes as a boat trader ... broker, he calls it. Boat brokerin' seems to be a pretty good game to be in."

"Except that you and I know his level of brokering couldn't be."

"Right. Too many old boats and not enough of them. Now where does all that moolah come from?"

"Beats me. I sprung smuggling on him and that's what got me jacked up a while ago."

Cal raised his colorless eyebrows. "That's what I been thinkin' but I don't know."

"Ever shake him down after one of his jaunts?"

"Sure have and drawed a blank four times. After that many blanks a man begins to look silly."

"I guess so. You have any other ideas?"

Lane shrugged. "I got all sorts of ideas, but they don't get me nowhere."

Johnny eyed the other hard. "You don't raise a lot of fuss on your job, Cal. Did Erico oppose you last election?"

The sheriff grinned. "He sure did."

"Then you're not in his debt. What exactly are you looking for, Cal?"

The man's eyes seemed as placid as a lake. "Oh … one thing and another. Among 'em is a forty-five pistol what killed a man. Another is a fella that manages to get liquor from Cuba to Florida. A hell of a lot of liquor."

"More than Griff could bring in his boat?"

"Sure. 'Specially when he always comes in empty. Somehow I'd like to get a look at Renfrow's Island."

"Why Renfrow's?"

"Number of reasons. Griff's boat has been spotted in that area three times."

"Why don't you go see old man Renfrow?"

"Because he don't take kindly to visitors. Besides his island is beyond territorial waters. He's a hard old man too. Just as soon shoot you and call you a prowler as not. He's done it and gotten away with it."

"Who's on the island besides him?"

"A wife who's big as me'n you."

"How does he make a living?"

"He made it when rum running was safer and worth more money."

"What makes it worth anything now?"

"Well, we're about to tax whiskey into the shades. Pay more taxes than the likker's worth. Bootleggin' is gettin' to be a high payin' occupation again."

"You think he'd still be interested in bootlegging?"

"He must get bored as hell out there. He don't need the money, that's sure."

"What sort of guy is he?"

"Oh … a cantankerous old cuss with a beef a mile wide against ever'body and ever'thing. They sent him up for two years once and he come out all bitter and swearin' vengeance and I don't know what all."

Johnny grinned. "Maybe that's his idea of getting even … helping Griff."

"Could be easy enough, but that still don't tell how the stuff gets in. The Coast Guard would love to know the answer to that."

Johnny frowned. "I saw what looked like an old diving helmet when I was at Griff's. In the hallway. It was dark in there and it was just an impression. Maybe it was something else."

"Musta been. If you're thinkin' about him dumpin' the stuff and divin' after it that won't cook. Coast Guard's jumped 'im a dozen times but all he does is smile and offer 'em a drink. Don't kick up no fuss or nothin'. Just acts as nice as you please … and they didn't never find nuthin'."

Johnny scratched his head. "Since his trips don't make sense, then he must be decoying for something else … or someone."

"Thought of that, too, but it don't get you no place."

Johnny lit a cigarette and inhaled thoughtfully. "I'm looking for a gun that fired a forty-five bullet, too."

"What's that gun you got there?"

Johnny looked at it stupidly, then grew taut. "Damn ... *it's* one."

The sheriff grinned crookedly. "Sure it is, but you wouldn't find Erico carryin' no murder weapon. You can forget that angle."

Johnny slumped. "I guess you're right. Hell, I won't get any sleep here. Too much noise and visitors. I think I'll go out and snooze at Elf's place."

"What does Elf think about this business?"

"He's got some ideas, but he's about in our shoes. He doesn't know enough to do any good."

"Then you're satisfied we're on the same side?"

"Sure, Cal. Sorry about the way I've been acting. Jeff Wickware beat it out of me."

"Jesus ... Jeff licked you?"

Johnny chuckled. "Sure did and I got in the first lick. Jeff's a man and learned some stuff from the Japs that I'll stay a safe distance from, from now on."

"Damn ... I'da never thought it. Jeff's a good man all right, but ... Well, I figgered you'd be able to take two like 'im."

"I might after I learned what he was going to do, but as it stands now he cleaned my plow but good. That's the way it stays, too. Jeff's a good fellow."

"The best." The sheriff's eyes slitted. "How good do you know Jeff?"

"Not too well. I've ferried him over to Crane Cay occasionally. I've seen him several times. Why?"

"Oh ... nuthin', I was just wonderin'." With that vague answer he got up. "Well, tell Elf, howdy, for me."

"Sure will and I'll let you know what I find out ... if anything."

"All right and one other thing, Johnny. Why don't you tie up at Elf's place for a while?"

"At Elf's … why?"

" 'Cause I don't want to be lookin' for no more murder bullets for a while. This place is a plumb bushwhackers' paradise. All these boat sheds, warehouses and stuff. Some night with this place lit up a rifle'll crack somewhere back in the dark there and we'll be draggin' the bay for you. Erico is a proud, sensitive man and you sure ruined that pride this mornin'."

On his way to Elf's place Johnny thought soberly about Lane's advice. Now that Jeff and Larry had succeeded in thrashing and enticing a great deal of the bitterness from him, he could better appreciate it. Elf had advised him, too, but at the time he had been inclined to ignore it entirely. The thought of Larry tightened him and his hands gripped the wheel until his palms began to sweat. Johnny had always managed to find the best in women and having found it was usually successful in providing them with the best in entertainment. Larry was something quite out of his experience, save one person. Mari, with her jungle cat's body, her superbly rich coloring, her utterly amoral pursuit of her fleshly yearnings without the slightest heed to convention or codes. The flame of her love reached through time and seared him again, making an angry growl rumble in his throat. Larry was no better than she should be, he was certain of that. Yet he knew their experience of last night had opened a new world to her and he knew that her reaction was likely to be something different from any of her previous amorous explorations. She'd likely fall in love with him and he remembered that at several stages of their night together, he had forgotten the past enough to love her. Now that Mari had come back to him so vividly and unexpectedly, he felt guilty. Whatever leanings Johnny might have toward cleverly carven women they did not take him into the ignoble fields of unfair strategy and false-hoods of various shades. He preferred that Larry didn't fall in love with him; because as long as Mari stayed on the tapestry of his memory, no other woman could ever amount to more than temporary assuagement.

Elf was leaning against a coconut tree, slapping a long bladed knife negligently, but effectively, against the side of a rough shoe. "Hi, bub," he said spitting copiously.

" 'Mornin', Elf. What's new?"

"The mornin'," said Elf, with a dry grin. "Whut happened at Griff's?"

"Nothing except that I think I scared him mentioning those wet weather trips in his boat. He sicked Erico Pucci on me and I had to brush him around some."

Elf whistled a low note and sat in a canvas chair. "Ye don't care who you rough up, do ye?"

Johnny grunted. "Sheriff Lane's on my side."

Elf nodded abstractedly. "Make a good pall bearer all right 'cept he's too damn tall. Make it hard fer the other mens."

"He told me I ought to come out and pitch a tent with you."

"I been tellin' ye summa the same thing, but it ain't never reached ye."

"You wouldn't mind having me?"

"Nup. Ye don't talk a lot. Couldn't never abide a man what was always flappin' his jaws. Generally nothin' comes out but a lotta noise. I like it peaceful."

"I'll get a tent and pitch it ..."

"I got room and I ain't dirty." He spoke no more than the truth. His house was not elaborate by any conception of a recluse. His clothes were always clean and neatly pressed.

"I didn't mean that, Elf. I don't want to impose on you."

"Ye won't. Ye'll do the dishes and clean up ever' other day."

They discussed the proposed moving at some length, then after he had accepted Johnny asked, "I've got to know where Griff got that boat."

"Jeff probably didn't ast no questions when he bought it."

"No, he didn't. He was too glad to get it."

Elf spat quietly and looked across the blue waters of the bay. "Well, looks like ye'll hafta git sumpn else on Griff."

"That's what he's afraid of."

"Then it's a mortal cinch he's doin' sumpn' he ain't got no business to. Ye might follow him some day." Some day proved to be the next.

Day broke with leaden clouds low over the water sweating out a fine drizzle. The weather report spoke of a small storm center to the south and east, moving inland at ten miles an hour with winds of sub-hurricane force at its center so they knew the weather would last.

Elf took a last cup of coffee to the door with him and squinted landward. "Can't see half a mile," he muttered. "Griff'll come skatin' out o' Black River in another hour loggin' somethin' like twenty-five knots. Late this evenin' or tonight he'll come draggin' in at three or four knots. That's somethin' fer ye to chew over."

Johnny massaged the back of his head, moving the wavy masses of brindled hair. "Goes out fast and comes in slow ... Maybe he's waiting for dark to set in."

"Does it night or day. No matter when he comes in he's crawlin'. Ever listen to a strainin' motor?"

"Plenty of times. His motor straining when he comes in?"

"Not 'zactly. Still and all if it was turnin' over that fast ordinarily he'd be makin' ten knots."

Johnny thought for a while. "A load'd make it do that."

"Sure it would, only he don't never have any load. Maybe we better be gettin' on out a ways and pick him up."

"All right. You got any binoculars?"

"Got a pair of Zeiss eight by fifties."

Johnny grinned. "They might do. I have a pair of binos and Dad's old brass spyglass."

"Got any shootin' irons?"

"Why?"

"Oh well, we might want to shoot a skipjack or a whale or sumpn."

"I got all we'll need."

"Just the same I'm takin' my ole hawg leg. Don't no other gun feel right in my hand."

CHAPTER NINE

ELF and Johnny cruised in small slow circles and waited in vain. Either Griff had decided to forego the trip or he had slipped them. After circling for two hours, they decided to call it a day, because the water had become rough with a ground-swell that showed promise of getting worse. The wind whipped the tops off whitecaps and sent sheets of spray driving over the rails of the *Snorter*. Their oilskins were some protection, but by the time they came in sight of Elf's island they were soaked to the skin.

There was another boat tied at Elf's wharf, one they couldn't identify, but there was no one in sight.

"Know the boat, Elf?"

"Nup. Never seen it before. Where's the owner?"

"Don't see anyone. Maybe he invited himself into your shack."

"Then he c'n invite hisself out. This ain't no railroad station."

As they neared the shack Griff Griggs stepped out clad in a long green plastic slicker with storm hat to match. He beamed at them genially grinning from ear to ear. "Well, well. Step in out of the rain, gentlemen. Been fishing?"

"Huntin'," replied Elf shortly. "You want sompn'?"

"Sure ... Johnny, hows for me and you to have a little talk ... private like?"

"Suits me. This is Elf's house so we can't ask him to leave."

"Didn't have any such thought. Let's go aboard my cruiser."

Johnny nodded and they walked down the slope to the wharf. As soon as they were out of earshot Griff clapped Johnny on the shoulder. "Johnny, I'm a live and let live man. I believe in it like a religion. I like people who live and let live."

"That makes you crazy about yourself, I suppose."

Griff laughed. "Well, that's not what I came out here for. I'd like to be a friend of yours and I think the first friendly act would be to tell you something that might save you trouble."

"Like what?"

"You're a curious man. Stop being curious."

"Why?"

"Because it might not be the thing to do. Here, step in. It's dry and comfy. What about a drink?"

"No thanks." Johnny followed Griff into the cabin and took a seat. "All right, Griff, get on the line."

Griff's grin was a little stiff. "I can see where you might want to get the man who did your father in and I don't blame you. I didn't do it and I don't know who did." The grin faded entirely and the face became hard. "All right, I'll get on the line. Don't start smelling out my tracks."

"Ultimatum," said Johnny softly, his lips twitching with a smile. "First a politician, then an ultimatum. What sort of racket are you in, Griff?"

"Who said I was in a racket at all?"

"Anyone in a legitimate business isn't concerned who knows about it and they don't send men like Erico Pucci around to try to intimidate respectable citizens."

Griff's broad face darkened. "Just the same I don't want you nosing around in my business. I'm telling you as a friend, but this is the last time I'm telling you."

"Why didn't you go out this morning, Griff. It's perfect for your ... er trips."

"That's none of your business. Got any more questions?"

"Yes. Why do you speed out and drag back when you go on a trip?"

Griff's face turned the color of putty. "You talk a lot, Johnny," he gritted, his jaw thrust forward. "Just be careful you don't talk too much. Now get off my boat."

"Behave, boy," said Johnny ominously, getting to his feet. "I'll get off the boat when I get goddamned good and ready. I've been wanting to look this boat over." He turned and started toward the stern bilge cover when he heard the sudden movement of the big man. He glanced back and found the round steady eye of a .38 automatic staring at him.

"Off the boat, Johnny. I'd just as soon let you have it as not."

"Yeh … and me too." Elf's voice was as rough as sharkskin. "Drop that there popgun and turn around. I'd just as leif blow a hole in ye I could put my foot in."

Griff went as pale as milk, but he dropped the gun and faced about to see Elf holding an enormous .45 on him with a steady hand.

Johnny walked up, his face red with rage, and slapped the big man as hard as he could. Griff reeled, lost his balance and crashed into a bulkhead shaking the craft like it had struck a reef. "Next time you pull a gun on me, Griff, you'd better use it."

"I will," said Griff shaking with humiliation. "You can depend on it."

"I see you don't carry forty-fives no more," said Elf, picking up the .38 and tossing it into the ocean.

Griff's face went blank. "I never carried a forty-five."

"That so? Who'd you give that'n to you bought at Brakeley's some time back?"

"Who said I bought one from Brakeley's?"

"I say so. What'd ye do with it?"

"Just try to find out," he snarled.

"Oh, I'll try all right," said Elf winningly. He hefted the big gun in his hand and with a tilt of his head to Johnny, spat copiously on the spotless cabin floor and stepped out on deck and thence to the wharf.

The cruiser muttered briefly, then took off, its stern hidden in a smother of foam.

"How did you know he bought a gun from Brakeley's?" asked Johnny, his hands tensely clenched.

"Oh, I been nosin' 'round. Went to Lake Springs and nosed a little, then down to Wakalla, then back in the Glades to Simp Ellis' old store. Simp's one o' them men what don't know time is flyin'. He got stuff in that store he never finds lessen a rat digs it out. Said he had been to Brakeley's one day and seen Griff buy a second hand forty-five, so I went to ast Brakeley about it, but he's scairt o' his own shadder, so I had to tell him I'd make Cal Lane talk for me if he didn't come across, then he got out his book … swore he had plumb fergot but there it was. Mighty nigh shook to pieces when I ast him about it. Scairt all the time. Begged me not to tell Griff he showed me the book."

"Come to think of it, Cal is looking for a forty-five automatic, too," said Johnny remembering his conversation with the sheriff.

"Yeah. Truck farmer got killed with it. Man never done nuthin' to nobody in his life. Mild sort of a cuss with a big family. Me'n Cal figger he musta seen somethin' he didn't orta and either got plugged to make him quiet or he tried to put the black on somebody. That slug is the onliest clue. No motive."

"Who was it?"

"Fella name of Trask, Thornton Trask."

"What happened to his family?"

"They're out there in the edge of the Glades with a levied off twenty-five acres of land, still truckin'."

"How do you get there?"

"Down Black River past ... Now what you got in yer bonnet?"

"I think I'll talk to the widow."

"Well, she didn't know nuthin'. He hadn't tole her a thing seems like."

"If he'd been preparing to put the screw on someone he might have mentioned something slyly that she forgot. I think I'll take Cal with me."

"Good idea. Might save ye from a bushwhackin'. Think I'll go 'long too. Say, you'n Cal both totin' a forty-five slug apiece. Ever try to find out if they come from the same gun?"

Johnny started. "By God, I never thought of that. It would be an outside chance, but I'm going to see. Where does Cal send his ballistics problems, Jacksonville?"

"Nup. Got a retired gun nut here name of Phillips. He used to work for the Canton Police Department. Good at stuff like that."

"That's a break. I'll talk to Cal."

The water grew rougher as the day waned and a fair gale was blowing. Elf sat near the door spitting occasionally into the darkness and Johnny lay at full length on the floor drowsing, thinking of Mari and Larry, but as usual Mari routed Larry and Johnny squirmed and cursed under his breath. He'd have to tell her but he didn't relish the thought. By keeping his mouth shut there might be more of that delightful association before love reared its head. He had no doubt that she'd be hurt and probably angry at him. He grinned to himself. He was taking a lot for granted and making some rather egotistic assumptions.

His mind was relatively at peace and verging on slumber when the ripping slam of slugs tore through the grail tin and packing board walls of the shack. Elf froze for an instant, then tumbled backward just as another burst showered them with dust, broken glassware and mud dauber's nests.

Three times more the deadly hail of submachine gun fire criss-crossed the hovel, then silence.

With a spring that belied his age, Elf leaped to a light switch, threw it, caught his revolver on the run and ducked out of the back door. Johnny risked a peek and there, in the glaring lights of the wharf, rode a cruiser pitching in the high waves with a man standing in the afterdeck with a sub-gun striving desperately to clear a stoppage ... Then Elf's big gun began to boom like a small field piece. A piece of the taff-rail kited upward by one of the big slugs struck the gunner, making him lose the fresh clip he was trying to load. Another smashed the glass in the wheelman's face and still another one thudded sickeningly into something soft.

Johnny came into the fray with Elf's old pump gun and began to ladle out a hail of buckshot spraying the cruiser from bow to stern. The wheelman ducking as low as he could yanked the throttle and the cruiser sank low as the powerful propeller dug in. He whirled the craft about and in a matter of seconds had disappeared into the murk and rain.

"Well, I thought they had you that time, Elf."

"Woulda if I hadn'ta fell over. Don't see how I got sandwiched that first spurt. You hurt?"

"No. Did you get any of them?"

"Yup. Didn't you hear that there *thwuck?* Didn't sound like nuthin' but meat t'me."

"What do you think they'll do with him?"

"Ask God. Mebbe they'll dump him back in the Glades and let the crocks git 'im. 'Tain't likely that they'll beat the bushes lookin' fer a doctor. Them things has to be reported. Let's try to clean up some o' this here mess else we'll wake up wuth a shiv o' glass in our asses."

Morning dawned cool and with that bell like clarity that follows the washing action of a storm. As far as the eye could see, seaward wave-horses raced too and fro, shaking their white foamy manes that caught the suns rays, making a vast expanse of snowy crests in the deep blue.

Johnny had gotten up early and after a quick breakfast raced the *Snorter* across the bay to Crane Cay, beating clouds of spray from the waves which still tossed high from the nights blow. As he swerved up to the wharf and killed his engines, Larry came running down the hill in her black velvet shorts with white trimming and a little whiff of a jacket. She ran with the long free stride of youthful health, her long deliciously curved legs flashing golden in the morning sun, her inky hair glinting as it whirled about her shoulders.

"I didn't see how you could go another day without even saying good morning," she said breathlessly as she came up.

He grinned at her. "I'm sorry I've had breakfast."

"What?" She was off balance for a moment.

"I'm full. As much as I'd like to eat you, I can't make it this morning."

"Oh … idiot." Her eyes grew serious. "Johnny, I'm glad to see you."

His own seriousness matched hers. "Come aboard, Larry. I wanted to see you, too."

She stepped aboard the *Snorter* and went below, taking a seat on the plastic covered lounge. Her eyes sought his hopefully. "You wanted to see me?"

"Yes …" He seemed at a loss.

"Johnny, the other night … It was something special to me."

He nodded. "And to me, too."

"Then you feel it too? I mean …"

"Don't say any more, Larry. I know what you're driving at and I'd like to save you some chagrin and maybe regret. The other night was wonderful. You drew me further out of myself than anyone has in a long time. I admire you immensely; and, but for one thing, I'm sure I'd be in love with you. Do you want to hear a story that you've known all along must be in back of my head?"

"Yes, Johnny. Tell me."

He told her of Mari, of her gold and ebony glory, of her restless savage passions and exhorbitant capacity for love, her total all-giving philosophy and the way she worshipped him with every fiber of her being, with every atom of her soul.

When he had finished she raised her head and her eyes were wet. "A woman in love, Johnny, is supposed to be a clawing scratching bitch, but I'm going to be an exception to the rule. I understand now and I know I could never hope to equal her. For one reason, I couldn't give you what she could have. For another I'd always come up short … But you say she's gone, you'll have to forget her some day."

"I know, I know. I tell myself that. Members of my family who resented the fact that she was an honest straightforward pagan have told me so in a few million chosen words. A few girls have pointed it out. Girls who have none of your refreshing objectiveness and honesty. All logic points to the fact that I must forget her and start anew." He shrugged. "Yet no one has told me how I'm to do it, so their advice doesn't do a lot of good."

"They're not involved as deeply as you," she said softly, her breasts throbbing with one vast ache. "It's easy to sit on the sidelines and make profound observations all loaded with reason and logic."

"Yes, that's the way it goes. I'm just as guilty as the next one, I suppose. Well, there it is, Larry. I thought it best that you know."

"Of course it is. It's better now that I know, else I'd have thought you were one of those men who feel that after a girl has given all she isn't worth loving."

He smiled faintly. "I never really knew what love was until Mari had given all … and it didn't take her long to convince me. I was afraid at first because she was such an intense creature. I never saw anyone who lived at half her voltage." His eyes grew misty and his voice was husky. "She took a knife and nicked her ears once and made love to me rabidly, like a blue white gas flame … and wherever she caressed me she left a trail of blood until I was smeared with her. Blood all over me, blood salty on my tongue, the perfume of it in my nostrils, my hands and body sticky with it. From me it was transferred back to her. I never saw anyone bleed so much from such tiny wounds … but she quit bleeding when we stopped … just like she had willed it to stop."

Larry was breathless and taut listening to him. "Johnny, maybe she willed it to bleed as well as to stop. That sounds a little weird, but it could be true."

He nodded sadly. "With her anything could be true."

Larry sighed tremulously, feeling a relief she could not understand. Was love to her something that rode into being on the wings of passion and flew away after the object proved unavailable? She put her question into words, but he shook his head. "No, it couldn't be that. Unavailability is something that usually intensifies longing. It doesn't reduce it. Maybe you're so healthily constituted that you're too well balanced to let something like this throw you off."

"I like to hear you say it whether it's true or not," she said with a smile. "For a while I was afraid I'd curl up and die and I think the way you told that story, the way you looked telling it, frightened me. I know what you'd expect and I know just as well that I couldn't provide it."

He smiled and with a gesture dismissed everything. "Where's Jeff?"

"He'll be over tonight. He's bringing a party. Why don't you come. Might as well expose yourself a little. It won't hurt you."

"I think I will," he said easily. "I guess I'd better dress though."

"Don't dress."

"Okay. You know, that Jeff's quite a guy. There's the man for you, Larry."

She nodded. "I've thought about him. He's a great guy, a generous thoughtful person all loaded with two handed extravagance ... He doesn't affect me physically, possibly because I've never thought of him in that way since the first day we met."

"Well, give it some thought. I'll see you later in the day. I have a lot of running around to do."

CHAPTER TEN

HE had seen Cal Lane, borrowed his bullet and had taken them both to Phillips, the ballistics expert. Then he had gone out to the island, picked up Elf, and the two of them returned to town to see the sheriff.

"Got some news for you," Cal said, after Johnny and Elf were in his office. "Phillips didn't have nothing to do; so he went to work on them bullets. They came from the same gun."

Johnny grew taut. "We're getting closer, Cal."

"Seems as if. What you gonna do, now?"

"I'm going to see the Trask family."

"I talked to them. They don't know anything."

"I'm going anyway. They might have remembered something. Maybe you ought to come along."

"Not a bad idea. You comin', Elf?"

"Sure. I'm in on this here thing now. Havin' me some fun fer a change."

The *Snorter* stuttered slowly down Black River and the farther they went the denser became the jungle that was the Everglades. "How does anyone make a living down here," asked Johnny.

"Richest land in the world. A syndicate came down here and cleared this spot and levied it, then went busted before they had a chanct to use it. Trask bought it at a sheriff's sale. He done right well."

Lane nodded in agreement. "Wasn't a wrong thing the man ever done in his life. Quiet hard worker and a good family man. Didn't never plague nobody."

They came suddenly on a clearing where a large rambling house fronted the river. There seemed to be a small army of children in the big front yard and all came streaming down to the landing to inspect the *Snorter,* which was a bigger craft than they were accustomed to seeing on that part of the river.

Elf stepped out on the rickety landing and started saying howdy to all of them. Cal and Johnny followed him.

"Son," Cal said to the biggest boy, a strapping youngster of twelve or thirteen. "Is your ma to home?"

"Yes, sir. You want to see her?"

"Yep, we all does," said Elf.

Ten minutes later they were seated on the broad verandah sipping cups of black pungent coffee.

"Mrs. Trask," said Johnny at length, "the sheriff questioned you, I know, after your husband's death and you could tell him nothing. We now know that the same gun he was shot with also shot my father. I'm just wondering if maybe you hadn't remembered something now that things have quieted down."

Mrs. Trask, a big capable woman with work hardened hands and a strong handsome face, frowned and nodded. "Yes, I do remember something, Mr. Elgin. I was too upset to remember it, Cal ... I'm sorry."

"Better late than never," he said. "What was it?"

"Well, the day before Thorn was killed he had boat trouble and took a short cut through Indian Creek. It's just a little thread of water, you know. He always dragged a pirogue and that put him only half a mile from the house. When he got here he was a little excited about something, but he just brushed me off when I asked him about it."

"What did he say," asked Johnny, leaning forward eagerly.

"Nothing much. He just laughed it off and said maybe we'd have a new Chris Craft before long ... for free. That was the end of it and I never thought about it any more until one day a week or so ago it all came back to me."

"Then you think it might have been something he saw coming through Indian Creek that made him say that?"

"Maybe. I remember now that I thought at the time he was just wishing. He did that sometimes. He'd get the catalogue some time and him and the kids would sit down and order all sorts of stuff. Of course, they never sent the orders off. Just sort of a game."

"He must have seen something," said Cal, wiping the sweat band of his old Stetson. "Nobody had anything against him."

"Well," said Johnny, with a grin that was not nice to see, "that's what I wanted to hear. Indian Creek, here I come."

"Here *we* come," said Elf. "Ye need a helper."

"You do have your uses," admitted Johnny touching the back of his head gingerly. "When shall it be, at night or in broad daylight?"

"Why not fly over it?" said Cal.

"Doesn't give time for close examination and we don't know what we're looking for."

"And," put in Elf caustically, "ye ain't gittin' me in none o' them danged contraptions."

As they nosed out of the bayou into open water a sleek cruiser ashine with brilliant lacquer and spotless brass swerved and bore down on them. It slowed and came alongside.

Jeff Wickware stepped out of the cockpit and faced them from the afterdeck. "Hey, Johnny, I've been looking for you. Would you know that cruiser of your dad's if you saw it?"

"A mile away," said Johnny with a curious exultance.

"Busy right now?"

"No."

"Come over to Crane Cay. Alf and I have two cruisers there that Jesse is putting in shape. One of them is unusual."

Johnny could hardly restrain a yell. "I'll be there in no time. You want me to drop you, Cal, or do you want to see this, too?"

"Hell, I want to see," said Cal.

"Okay then. Hold your teeth."

"And he ain't funnin' neither," muttered Elf as he grabbed a stanchion and held on for dear life. The *Snorter* roared, spouted a spray of water from her exhausts, turned and leaped forward sending up twin sheets of spray from her sharp prow. Like an arrow shot from a bow, the big boat raised out of the water until it seemed she was almost flying, smashing waves and sending up showers of water that stung the face like bird shot.

As they approached Crane Cay, Johnny turned the nose of the *Snorter* toward the southern tip and swung her inshore as close as he dared.

"There they is," yelled Elf, pointing.

Johnny reduced throttle and gave a good look at the cruiser that rode at anchor in the quiet protected little bay. The one that had been dragged up on the beach on rollers he scarcely glanced at. The other one took and held his attention for a minute, then he opened the throttles and headed back toward the speck that was Jeff following in the distance. He hadn't been able to keep up with the fleet *Snorter*.

"What do you think, Johnny?" yelled Jeff, when Johnny pulled alongside.

"It's her all right. Where did you get it?"

"Jesse bought both boats for me. He got them from a swamp rat name of Martell."

"Thanks, Jeff. Thanks a lot. I'll check with you."

Again the *Snorter* roared into life, leaped into the waves and soon disappeared in a cloud of spray.

There were seven people at the party that night besides Jeff, Larry and Johnny. Johnny had come late, dressed coolly in slacks and a white sport shirt, but no one else had dressed either so he did not feel conspicious.

As soon as they could, after introductions, Johnny and Jeff went out on the roofless patio and sat in wrought iron chairs. Johnny seemed nervous and distrait.

"What did you get out of Martell?"

"Nothing, except that Griff had given him the boats. He was vague about why he had been the receiver of two boats, even bad ones. Griff, of course, won't remember where he got them and you can't make a man admit something like that, if he doesn't want to."

Jeff frowned and nodded. "You can't, of course. I wish you could."

Johnny told him of the projected trip to Indian Creek and of the reasons for it.

"I agree there. It has been suspected for some time that Griff runs contraband but so far no one has ever caught him at it."

"And that's the only way we'll ever get anything on him. Martell doesn't like Griff any more and I'm going to concentrate on him. I had the impression, so did Elf and Cal, that he was on the verge of telling something, but he never got around to it."

"Well, you have my best wishes, Johnny. If there is anything I can do, don't fail to tell me."

"You helped when you realized that cruiser might have been Dad's."

Jeff smiled. "That was Jesse. He noticed it and told me about it. I might never have noticed it because it's so badly in need of overhaul."

Johnny stood up. "Make apologies for me, will you? I got a hint of Mari from Martell and I'm antisocial. Elf and I are going to look at Indian Creek tonight or in the morning before day-light. I'll need the sleep."

"All right. Too bad you couldn't stay and help with the extra girls and I sincerely hope you learn more about Mari."

"Call in Jesse and Chris," said Johnny with a grin.

"Anna has appropriated Jesse and all Chris does is hang around and make moon eyes at Larry. He's smitten."

"Can't blame him," said Johnny. "She's lovely. Looks like you should take a fling there. You must be stone."

Jeff grinned. "I give the impression, but I'm not really. Goodnight, Johnny."

The three stag girls were in a group gossiping and for a moment Jeff stood in the door and tried to remember their names and failed. He shrugged and went to Larry who had skipped the party and was sitting in a beach chair on the front lawn. He walked over and took a chair beside her.

"Bored?"

She sighed and wriggled deeper into the chair. "No. Just peaceful and a little sad."

"Sad? Why?"

She sighed again and felt a rush of tears sting her eyes. "I fell in love with Johnny and got told in a nice way that it wouldn't cook. I wasn't as badly done in as I might have expected, but it isn't very conducive to soaring happiness. Jeff, did you know his girl, Mari?"

"No. She must have been something."

"She was. Johnny told me about her and just hearing him tell it made her immortal. You should have heard him."

Jeff was quiet for a while. "What, if any, thinking have you done about the future."

She wriggled and stretched luxuriously. "None. That's one of the relieving features of this place. I don't have to think about anything. Is there any hurry?"

He chuckled. "None at all. You're a good thing to have around. I'm sort of getting used to the idea. You can stay as long as you wish."

"You've been swell about this, Jeff. I was certain you'd come in some night and ask me to sleep with you."

"Disappointed?"

She laughed. "No ... Pride pricked a little. You seem impervious to my charms."

"That's hardly true. I still have a lot of unfinished business on the mainland. If I were about everyday, things might be different."

"We're frank about it anyway, aren't we."

"I think it's the only way to be. It's a change from the sort of thing one comes to expect from a crowd like the one in the house."

"Where do you pick them up?"

"At Macklins. I passed the other day and they put in a bid for a party over here, so I said okay. They gathered the rest."

"Why do you do it, Jeff? You don't care for it."

"It's fun sometimes. This one tonight is a bore, however. I'll be glad when they leave."

"Who ferried them over?"

"I did and I'm ready to ferry them back as soon as they get too drunk to protest. The time approacheth, I think. Excuse me and I'll go see what I can do to get them started."

Larry sat perfectly still in her chair, her mind carefully blank. In spite of the blankness a creeping tide of pure sensuousness began to premeate her until at last she was driven to full consciousness by the wanton drive of throbbing passion. She decided to take a walk to ease the tightness in her loins.

She was not consciously following Anna and Jesse, but somehow she found herself, half an hour later, watching them shamelessly, hidden from view by a growth of brush.

"You know, Anna," he was saying, "I like a lot of things about you."

"Like what, Jesse?" Her voice was husky, with a delectable tremble.

"Like you … all of you." He inched closer, taking his time.

Anna licked her lips and slowly put her leg down, but the dress stuck halfway up the thigh. "I like you too, Jesse.

"How much?"

"I don't know yet … But a lot, I think."

She grew weary of his slow advance and with an increased rate of breathing she sat up and her arms went out meeting him more than half way. She writhed in his powerful grip that was not powerful enough to restrain her, because Anna, too, was strong. Now she was stronger than ever.

With a heave that spoke well for the strength of his back, Jesse put her on her feet and the embrace was even closer than before. Anna could not be still and Jesse was enjoying the strength she exhibited. He drew his lips from hers. "I think we'll get along," he said huskily, dropping his hands down below her waist, bringing her in close to him.

"Oh, Jesse," she whispered. "Hold me closer … closer." Her hips, acting of their own will, drove out smothered exclamations which Jesse matched as he found her lips again.

Under his long facile fingers her skirt started to rise in slow jerks creeping up her long fine thighs like a live thing, giving the moon a chance to wash fresh inches each moment in its pure light. A curious little note forced its way past both their lips. She tore her mouth from his and with both hands ripped the shirt open and gave him access to her breasts, sprouting high as she arched herself back. He did not need a second invitation. The dress ceased its upward movement momentarily. Heated murmurs started from her depths as his lips drove her frantic with their attacks on the peaks, that were rigid from the action of his lips.

The dress mounted again and when it stopped she was bare from the waist down save for the skimpy panties that blushed pinkly in the white light. Her legs were marvelously sculptured posts of powerful muscle clothed in skin of such ineffable fineness. His hands played lovingly with them even as his lips devoured the sweetness of her breasts.

"Jesse, Jesse ..." She buried her face in the curve of his neck and bit the skin holding it in her teeth, pulling at it with her lips that seemed determined to make a meal of him.

Larry bit her lips as her muscles contracted, making her limbs twitch, fresh sweat breaking out on her forehead.

His hands had reached Anna's briefs and was drawing them slowly downward stopping occasionally to make short, but objective journeys that drove muffled cries from her mouth. Pink briefs described a quick arc in the air and hung by the elastic waist band from a nearby bush.

Anna held him close, her breasts drinking in the sensation of resting without obstacle against his smooth chest. Slowly she swept them across him, her throat set and corded in the moonlight against the urgency of her vocal cords striving to sing out some note of the slaughtering tides that were sweeping her continually.

Larry wiped her eyes and rested her forehead on her arm for a monent, but looked quickly up as a shrill hissing note tore itself from Anna's lips. They were still standing, still close, but there was a difference. They stood as though transfixed by the same spear, impaled into immobility by the same agency.

Then almost reluctantly, a separate, but related little motion was born to both of them, a motion that soon took on time and tempo, and was punctuated by a throaty gurgle that was musical and rhythmical, rising higher and higher in the scale, then was abruptly cut off as for a second they held still.

"Jesse ... She mouthed his lips and neck and ears, her hands fluttering about with approaching frenzy. "Jesse ... I knew it ... I knew it'd be like this ... this ..." Jesse dropped his hands below her waist filling them with her firm bounteous flesh urging her closer.

She contorted herself in a magnificent upsurge of frightening muscular power, hooked her heels behind his as they hung balanced precariously in a cataleptic embrace. Slowly they started to fall but their only reaction was to grip each other tighter. The sand received them with a soft thud.

For a long time they lay still and as they lay relaxed now, but still as close as possible, Larry rose shakily to her feet and crept away, staggering a little, her loins thudding with heavy thrusts of stormy blood, her face and arms damp. The skin of her thighs was so sensitive that an errant blade of grass, raking upward as she stepped over it made her almost cry out.

CHAPTER ELEVEN

FROGS slowed their croaks as the night wore on and by the time Elf and Johnny nosed the light skiff into Indian bayou they had hushed for the night. A brave wildcat mewed harshly on the southwest bank and a gar splashed sleepily just ahead of the bow. For a mile they paddled silently straining their eyes for something that would give away what Trask might have spotted.

Elf stopped paddling and spat in the water. "I been thinkin'."

"Thinking what?"

"What could Trask've seen that nobody else did? Trask ain't the onliest man that uses Indian Creek."

Johnny stopped paddling and straightened up. "Now you just said something. Does Indian Creek have any tributaries?"

"Dozens of 'em. Trask wouldn'ta used none of 'em unless he seen somethin' that made him git curious. He'da took Indian Creek proper if he was takin' a short cut home."

"And that might be any tributary and unless we saw what he saw we're out here whistling in the dark."

"Yeh … and astin' t' git ourselves shot. This here ain't no good, Bub. Le's go on home and try t' do some better thinkin' than we done before we decided on this jackass trip."

They turned about and paddled out to Indian Creek into Black Bayou. They stopped paddling as they drew abreast of Griff's place, looked searchingly, then continued another mile until they reached the *Snorter* and tied the skiff astern. Johnny kicked the big engines into life and nosed the craft carefully along until they reached open water.

Dawn was beginning its early painting efforts when they reached Elf's wharf.

Elf fixed a hearty breakfast of broiled ham, eggs and hot biscuits with his particular brand of coffee which was like a shot in the arm after a night among the damp mists and insects of the Glades.

"Well," said Johnny as he lit an after breakfast cigarette, "what do we do now?"

Elf shrugged, his little eyes lighting with humor. "You astin' me? I thought this here was yo' show."

Johnny grinned. "It *was* my show, but you've taken it away from me and you've done about all the smart headwork that's been done so far."

"Right now the headwork is done tooken a slump. Don't pear like there's nuthin' to do but set and wait for a break."

"And that's what I don't like."

A chill wind blew in from the north an hour later and with it came the formation of fog that started like a low lying blanket hiding the waves. Through it Elf could see the prow of a battered old cruiser that putted contentedly along, headed straight for their island.

It was a mile and a half away when the fog closed in and blotted out everything. Close on the thickening of the mist there came to their ears the racketing chatter of an automatic weapon. In a flash Elf was handing Johnny the shotgun and thrusting his revolver into his waistband.

"Hit it, boy. Ain't but one outfit around here what's got a chopper and whoever they're shootin' at is bound to be on our side.

Seconds later the *Snorter* bellowed and surged away from the wharf and was swallowed instantly in the fog.

From their closed in view, the fog wasn't as thick as it seemed from the island, but it was thick enough to cause concern … to Elf, at least, because the *Snorter* was charging into the teeth of the mist smashing waves to fragments, the engines booming out a mighty song of power.

"Ease her back, bub," yelled Elf. "Seems like this was about the spot where I last seen that old boat."

Johnny had hardly cut the throttles when the craft wallowing dead in the water loomed out of the cottony atmosphere and only by fast wheel action did Johnny avert a collision.

"Whew," breathed Elf. "That'n was close. Back 'er down."

They had gone past and now in reverse they had to search for the other vessel. They found it still drifting but noticeably lower in the water.

Johnny warped in close and Elf leaped to the slippery fore-deck, made his way aft to the cabin into which he ducked only to pop up again. "Tail 'er around, bub," he called. "We got a tow job and we gonna hafta do it fast else she'll go down. This here is a job fer the Coast Guard."

It was a nightmarish chore towing the stricken wallowing boat at high speed through the thick fog. She had taken in so much water that it was Elf's opinion that the faster they towed her, the action tending to lift the bow, the less water she'd take in.

"Sounds like a Coast Guard foghorn over to port, bub," yelled Elf. "Ease over thataway."

They picked up the cutter as it was nosing carefully out and Elf screeched at them, pointing to the half sunken boat.

The cutter picked up speed, made a sharp turn and was soon alongside. "What's all this, Elf," roared the officer in charge.

"Shootin' scrape out on the sound. Where kin this tub be beached? Bottom's out of 'er."

"Follow the cutter. We'll pull her up on the ramp." The cutter surged ahead and by the time they reached the ramp the landing was alive with men. Johnny leaped back, slashed the line and whirled the *Snorter* aside leaving it to Elf and the others to get a line on her and winch her out of the water.

An hour later, Johnny and Elf sat in the office of the grizzled old veterans of many a bad blow and a war. Cal Lane was there, too, sitting silent, but alert.

"That's all there is to it," said Elf who had the floor. "We seen the boat cornin' in … headed straight for my place, then the fog moved in and right after that we lost sight of 'er. We heered the goldangdest chatter … just like the other night when they mighty nigh cut my shack in two."

There was a general stiffening and raising of eyebrows.

"How come you didn't report it, Elf?" asked Cal mildly.

Elf sniffed. "And what'd ye of done? We couldn't identify 'em and they didn't do nuthin' but bust up twelve dollars and six bits worth of china and a coupla ole iron skillets."

"That should have been reported, Elf," said Commander Earle. "You know that."

"All right," grumbled Elf. "I'm reportin' it now. You got the corpse o' Martell and a shot up boat. Whatcha gonna do about that?"

"Well, at the moment and with the lack of any evidence …"

"Same thing," snorted Elf. "Ye can't do nuthin' cause there ain't nuthin' to go on. Same thing."

A seaman came in holding a length of manila rope. "Sir, I took this off that old scow. Been towin' somethin'."

They took the rope and examined it but could find nothing out of the ordinary.

"Thanks, Dan, but all it is is a piece of new half inch manila rope. We'll keep it because it might tie up with something."

"Already been tied up with sompn'," beefed Elf bad temperedly. "Trouble is nobody knows what."

They detained Elf to tell them about the shooting, while Cal and Johnny went out and looked the old cruiser over. It had been holed repeatedly below the waterline and Johnny wondered how they had managed to get it to the mainland as full of water as it must have been. Cal was following his thoughts. "Musta strained the gizzard out of your boat pullin' dead weight like that."

"She was beginning to complain," admitted Johnny. "Who had something against Martell besides Griff Griggs?"

"If it was me," commented Cal soberly, "I'd consider Griff plenty. Musta been the same birds as shot up y'all's place the other night."

"Probably. Submachine guns are not too plentiful."

"Just for the hell of it," said Cal, opening an old stag handled barlow, "I'm gonna dig out a few of these slugs. You got a couple out of Elf's place and we'll let Phillips have them. One murder and one attempted murder connected up'll help each other."

"For a man investigating a murder, you're the calmest fish I ever saw."

Cal bent him a look of mild reproof. "What you want me to do, run around yellin' and wavin' my arms?"

Johnny chuckled. "That'd be worth traveling to see. I guess you know what you're doing."

"Well, now I don't know as I'd go that far. I'm doin' what I can. What you reckon that rope was tied to?"

"The one that seaman brought in?"

"Unh hunh."

"Your guess is as good as mine. Why?"

"Just wonderin'. It wasn't broken. It was shot in two."

Johnny massaged his jaw reflectively. "If it was an accident in the thick of the shooting then whatever was at the other end is still floating around."

"If it'd float," was the surprising reply. "If it was done on purpose they got whatever it was. What I don't like is it's a cinch Martell was comin' to see you; and since you say he almost talked the time you saw him, he must have been coming to talk."

"And maybe bringing something with him to back his talk up."

Cal shrugged. "Well, that may be, but we don't know."

Elf and Johnny made a cautious trip back through the fog without much conversation. As they tied the *Snorter* up Johnny asked. "If whatever that rope was tied to could float Elf, where would it be by now?"

Elf squinted and thought hard for a moment. "Be just about even with the island. I didn't dream that up. Been watchin' floatin' things around here for a long time. Tide one way she'd go one way. Tide the other way she'd go another. Now lemme see. Yap ... More or less right about out yonder."

They took Elf's boat because it was smaller; and though they combed the waters for a mile about the island and looked until their eyes ached, they could find nothing. The next morning early Elf swallowed a hasty breakfast and took a tour of the beaches coming back half an hour later, his face split by a big grin. "Well, I found it, begob, and it couldn't talk, but it told a lotta stories ... outa school, too."

Jeff Wickware came in sight just then, tied his gleaming cruiser up at Elf's wharf and walked to the shack.

"Hi, Johnny, Elf. Hear y'all had some excitement ... Damn, someone used a chopper on your shack, too."

"Yeah," said Elf, "with us in it, too."

Jeff shook his head. "This place is getting rough."

Elf grunted and closed one eye owlishly. "Could be, Jeff …
could be. What you after this mornin'."

"I'd like to speak to Johnny for a moment." They walked out
into the mist where Jeff faced the other.

"Johnny, Larry's in love with you."

Johnny's face grew bleak. "I know and I'm sorry as hell.
Larry's a beautiful kid and if it wasn't for one thing I'd probably
fall for her."

Jeff looked at him queerly. "According to Larry's own admis-
sion she's a lusty lover and enjoys her five senses. That or its
implication wouldn't stop you falling in love with her?"

Johnny's eyes grew stony. "What do you take me for
… eighteen ninety-seven? So far from stopping me, it very
nearly *made* me do it. For a few minutes in her company I nearly
forgot that I had a maggot in my brain that I'll never be able to
get out."

Jeff squirmed. "Maybe I'm a fool, but I wanted you to say
that. You see, I'm in love with her myself."

Johnny frowned. "I'll bet Larry never handed you anything
but the McCoy. Right?"

Jeff sighed. "So much the McCoy that half the time I find
myself wondering how anyone could be that way."

"You'd better make a move. I'm no authority on women, but
you'd better make a move and a good one or someone'll snap her
off like a marlin takes a nullet."

"Yes … I've been telling myself that very thing. For the first
time in my life I sort of stagger when I start to talk to her. I've
been busy all right, but not so much that I couldn't get home
every night. I'm scared, frankly."

"I think I can understand that. I guess if I wasn't tied down
by this thing I would have been scared of her, too. There's something unbelievable about her. Beauty, ouright animal magnetism,

charm, intelligence … and a nature that makes you shiver in retrospect once you've tasted it."

"And you've tasted?"

Johnny's eyes deepened and seemed to change color. "I've tasted. She'll tell you, if she figures you want to know. She's like that. Larry's as open faced as the city clock and you always know what time of day it is."

"I guess," said Jeff after a moment's silence, "I'd better get some courage."

"Scrape up all you can find, send Ole and family on a tour of the mainland and get about half plastered … Then watch out."

"Would you say she's promiscuous?"

Johnny spat angrily in the sand. "You sound like a school superintendent addressing the parents of a dilinquent."

Jeff blushed red. "Sounded pretty bad, didn't it?"

"Sounded stuffy and ordinary. She has a high riding nature. The difference is that hers demands a lot of attention. Other natures don't demand any, but I wouldn't have 'em at bargain prices."

Jeff nodded slowly and they started back toward the shack. "I have some good news for you, Johnny, and I wish I could give it to you. It happens that I can't."

"Then what the hell did you tell me for."

Jeff faced him. "Damn if I know, except that I think you're a good Joe and I hate to see you suffer."

Johnny went white. "Do you know what you're saying, Jeff?"

The other's eyes opened in astonishment. "Me … I didn't say anything. I just said I wish I *could* say it."

Johnny's nose flared like a mad stallion's. "Look, I …"

Jeff caught him by both forearms and squeezed certain points. A wave of shock flicked over him like a hot electric current and brought him back to earth.

"Sorry," said Jeff crisply. "I just can't say any more, now. It won't be long, Johnny. I promise it."

When he had gone Johnny sank into a chair white and shaken, sweat dropping from his face in a steady stream.

"Shook ye up some, 'pears like," commented Elf slyly.

"Shook me up, all right," quavered Johnny, his voice barely under control. "And he'd better know what he's talking about."

"Jeff most in generally does ... now who's the comp'ny. Damn place's gittin' to be a reg'lar cross road."

A slim grey launch pulled up to the wharf and Cal Lane got out and walked lazily toward them. "Mornin'," he said as though they had just met. "Seen Griff takin' off acrost the waters like a scared mud duck this mornin'. Sorta give me'n the Coast Guard some ideas."

Elf grinned. "Any ideas you'n the Coast Guard git'll come from me, and I don't aim to let the credit git lost in the shuffle. Looks like you'd be follerin' him to where he meets up with who-ever he meets up with."

"That ain't the problem," said Cal taking a canvas chair. "Problem's like it's always been. Where does he stow the stuff to bring it in?"

Elf grinned wider and stood up. "Come on over the dunes here, I got sompn' to show ye ... Johnny, ye didn't see it yet either. Jeff must of shook ye to pieces to fergit to ast me about it."

Johnny's face was too hard and set to change. "I forgot about it," he said stonily.

Twenty minutes walk brought them to an isolated stretch of beach and pulled half out of the water was a curious submarine shaped object. They gathered around it and examined it closely.

"See here," said Elf didactically. "This hatch screws off and look at the storage space in there." He took the hatch off and let them look. It was empty. The submarine like vessel was thirty feet long and five feet in diameter, but so light that they could move it easily. It was made of aluminum over a framework of the same metal. In a ring bolt at one end was a piece of new manila rope that had obviously been parted from the original piece by a bullet, the strands still dark from the metal of the projectile.

"That's yer answer," barked Elf, triumphantly.

Cal shook his head. "Nunh unh, Elf. Anyone could have seen a torpedo this size being towed behind a cruiser."

"Wrong again," said Elf patiently. "Damn if I ain't gonna run fer sheriff. I'm too smart to be a fishin' guide. Look at this hatch cover. See that there dial. Betcha them figgers feet of …" He cleared his throat. "Jesus, ye still don't git it? Feet of *submergence.*" Then he straightened up and looked at them triumphantly.

"Submergence," breathed Cal ecstatically. "That *might* be it."

"Might," snarled Elf, acidly. "That *is* it. How'd ye say Griff went out this mornin' … like a mud duck takin' off? All right, when you see him comin' back he won't be loggin' five knots. Cause why? Cause he'll be draggin' one o' these here contraptions loaded with whatever he wants t' bring in from scotch to heroin. Now put that in yer pipe and stick a match to it. Five foot's plenty deep when there's an overcast."

Johnny, stiff with a landslide of flogging emotions stood in his tracks without moving, without speech.

"Now, like I told you," pursued Elf, "mebbe you and the Coast Guard'll have something to talk about tomorrow."

Cal scratched his head. "Now where do you suppose he gets the stuff from?"

Elf suddenly went silent and with the cessation of conversation they straggled back toward the shack.

"So that's what Martell was bringing you, eh, Johnny?"

Elf answered for him. "That was it. Griff must have a better way of towin' it though. He must 'tatch it underwater. Bet ye again one o' them things got loose. Trask seen it. Mebbe pulled it back to Griff's place ... after he 'zammined it."

"We'll see," said Cal with satisfaction. "Y'all want to come along?"

"We'll be there," said Johnny, "in the *Snorter*."

Cal left them to their respective silences, but at length Johnny said, "When he wondered where the stuff came from, Elf, you shut up. Why?"

"Coupla reasons. If they knowed it come from Renfrow's island there ain't nuthin' they could do. Renfrow's island ain't owned by the 'Nited States. Renfrow owns it and they couldn't go bargin' in there."

"That's one reason."

Elf nodded abstractedly, but didn't mention the other one so Johnny prodded him. "What's the other reason?"

"A good'un. You're astin' too many questions. Time'll take care of it."

Johnny, sensitive now to all veiled remarks went taut. "You sound like Jeff now."

Elf spat at a darting insect bringing it tumbling into the sand. "Yap, mebbe I do at that."

The sun was not yet down, but it was hidden by low flying banks of clouds that had earlier in the day been fog.

CHAPTER TWELVE

COMMANDER EARLE had spoken to them earlier and relegated them to a position of watching, but though Johnny agreed in word, he intended to be in on the kill, if possible. There were too many things that might happen which could close Griff Griggs's mouth, and he wanted to avoid that, at all costs. So he lay to the south and brought the *Snorter* around on the extreme edge of a bank of fog that was rolling in. He peered into the dense grey mass and cursed under his breath. If Griff got the wind up and made a run for it, the fog was too close in and they'd lose him.

He jockied the *Snorter* out to sea for a short run, then brought her back in a course parallel to the fog. Out in clear water some distance away he saw the Coast Guard cutter cruising slowly out as though on a routine inspection then at a hissed exclamation from Elf he looked out to sea and saw Griff's huge cruiser making its slow way in. The fog crept in one flank while the cutter moved across off her course to intercept the incoming cruiser. Johnny continued his hovering tactics sticking half in and half out of the fog. Half an hour later all three boats had converged on the very lip of the fog bank.

Johnny, tense at the wheel kept his hands on the throttle still hanging back because he felt certain that Griff would not give up without some effort to fight or escape.

The cutter pulled in close now and stopped Griff not fifty yards from the edge of the fog which continued to creep in with a speed that was deceptive.

"All right, Johnny," said Elf. "Git on yer toes."

"I want to see what you're dragging, Griff," roared Commander Earle through a powered megaphone.

They didn't hear Griff's reply because at that moment a hatch flew open and a gun implacement slid smoothly into view. In a split second, the cutter was under the threat of the lean snouts of twin mounted fifty caliber machine guns, manned by a gunner who was obviously familiar with his weapons. Johnny, in a lightening glance saw that they had once adorned the turret of a bomber and were quite as deadly in the mounts now. Without a single thought save that the crew of the cutter was in deadly peril, he slammed the throttles open; and with a roar like the crack of doom, the long slender bow of the *Snorter,* lunging like a runaway whale, tore through the thin curtain of the fog and charged Griff's cruiser. So swift had been the change of the situation that the machine gunner was unable to bring his guns around and trip the triggers. The bow of the *Snorter* seemed to loom above him then came crashing in, flinging him overboard like a chip. Although the bow of the *Snorter* chewed and crushed the port rail through, it did not land a mortal blow to the cruiser. While Johnny was spinning the wheel madly to avoid crashing into the cutter, Griff opened his throttle wide and in a matter of seconds was lost in the fog, his speed showing that the shock or the crew had dislodged the submarine barge.

The *Snorter,* though it didn't crash into the cutter, did rub along side and managed to foul some cordage and gear which necessitated a few minutes work to free her. By that time Griff, roaring at full throttle through the fog, was out of sight.

"He's gotten away," mourned Commander Earle, as his men hacked away the mess caught on the *Snorter.* "Thanks a million, Johnny. He had us cold there, boy. A machine gun, no less, and who would have suspected it?"

"Me," barked Elf. "Mighta knowed he'd have sompn' like that."

Earle grinned. "I ought to put you on the payroll, Elf."

"Nup, all you want is them there fingerlin's with no hair on their lips. You don't want brains."

"I'm supposed to have the brains," said Earle, chuckling.

"Yap … I know you is, and jes' look whut happened."

Johnny's rudder had been bent in the crash and he was in a rage when he saw he couldn't operate the *Snorter* at more than quarter throttle.

"Whut you so all fired in a hurry about," said Elf slicing a chew from a fresh plug.

"I've been putting two and two together in the last day or so. Remember Martell telling me that I'd like to get my girl back?"

"Yap, and the bastard wouldn't drop another mumblin' word about it."

"Right. Well, he could have heard I was looking for her as well as the boats. It hasn't been exactly a secret. Then comes Jeff saying that I'll have some good news soon. I don't have Jeff catalogued yet, but there's something funny about him. How does he know I'll have good news soon? And if he knew they were out after Griff, then he couldn't have foreseen what happened to that deal and now maybe there won't be any good news unless I make it."

"Whut you talkin' about?"

"What do you think I'm talking about?"

Elf grinned and spat over the side. "Looks like ye might be talkin' about a little expedition."

"Right the first time but right now I got to use the Coast Guard ramp to get the kink out of that rudder."

The Coast Guard, always a cooperative organization, quite outdid themselves when Johnny asked for assistance. They were not unmindful of the fact that he had saved them from flying their flag at half mast.

Commander Earle summoned Johnny and Elf to his office. "Sit down, Johnny, Elf. Johnny, you haven't said so, but I have an idea you're going after Griff. Right?"

"Right, sir. Just as soon as I can get my boat in the water."

"Might I remind you what you could be running into … ?"

"Ye can tell 'im, but he won't pay ye no mind," put in Elf.

Earle smiled. "Just the same maybe I'd better tell him anyway. Johnny, Renfrow besides being a rum runner back in the days of my ensignship is an inventor and mechanic of no mean ability. It's ten to one that submarine barge is his idea from start to finish. Lane tells me he can't find Pucci … he went to pick him up …"

"What could he hold Pucci on?" interrupted Johnny.

"Those sub-gun slugs match. He thinks, and I agreed, that Pucci was behind that murder and that he shot up your shack or had it done. He's the only man in these parts who would import gunmen. Tommy guns around here are imports. Anyway, the chances are he's at Renfrow's with Griggs. We have reason to believe that Renfrow was violently bitter about his incarceration and vowed never to set foot on the mainland again. The island is his and we can't legally do a thing. Of course, we probably *could* but there would be questions asked and the red tape would reach from here to Washington … literally. Just between us girls, I'm glad you're going, but you needn't expect it to be a pushover. There are likely to be extra men there. Pucci's and those Griggs had around him. What else you find is any man's bet. They'll be well armed, surprisingly so, as you no doubt remember Grigg's armament. The man who handled that gun was an ex-gunner on a B-24. He knew his stuff. We pulled him out of the drink and that's our score. One man!"

"Has he talked?"

"Not a word, except that he dared us to try to take the island. I don't like the way he looked when he did, either."

"Well, we're going," said Johnny with a hard laugh. "Oh … Hello, Jeff. Where'd you come from."

Jeff shrugged lightly. "Oh, around. Where are you going?"

"We're going to take Renfrow's island."

"Damn …" He turned to Earle. "Charley, you approve of this?"

Commander Earle smiled wryly. "Seems he'll go whether I approve or not."

Jeff turned back to Johnny. "What do you have by way of armament?"

"Elf has a .45 and a shot gun."

Jeff frowned. "Don't be a fool, boy. You can't storm a place like that?"

"I don't have a private army and I see I'm going to have to *make* that good news you spoke of."

Jeff's face went grim. "Okay, I can't stop you, but I can go with you … and I can arm you properly."

A seaman came in with the news that the *Snorter* was seaworthy again and Johnny got to his feet. "I hate to be impatient but as a matter of fact, I am. Shall we be moving?"

Later in the day, Elf and Johnny stood and admired Jeff's "trophy" room. He seemed to have every sort of conventional weapon and any number of unconventional ones.

"Godamighty, Jeff, where'd ye git all these here weepons?"

"Here and there," said Jeff with a smile. "See one that strikes your fancy?"

"Sure do. Ain't seen a shootin' shape ole Winchester like this here'n in thutty year." He took down a beautifully preserved old 30-30 caliber lever action Winchester, flung the breech open and snapped the lever back in place. "If ye got any gas fer this'n I'll take it."

Jeff nodded, opened a marked drawer and pulled out two cartons of ammunition. "This be enough?"

Elf shook his head. "I ain't never been to waw and I don't know nuthin' about fire power, but three of them cartons ain't goin' t' weight me down none."

"Isn't this an M50 Reising," asked Johnny, picking up a slim deadly submachine gun.

"That's right. It's been fired maybe thirty times."

"What type of magazine does ... Oh, I see. I thought it had that original magazine that used to foul up. This one's all right."

"You seem to know your weapons, Johnny."

"A little. I'll take this if you don't mind."

"Take it. I'll take my old reliable, the Thompson, and a couple of drums."

"What's going on here?"

They turned to see Larry in a black velvet shorts ensemble and there was a collective indrawing of breaths.

She came on in. "All armed to the teeth and looking serious. What gives?"

They looked at each other and seemed by silent agreement to let Johnny explain. He told her in a very few words, then added, "We think we might find Mari there."

"Oh, Johnny, I'm so glad. I *really* am."

His eyes stung at the look on her face. "I know you are, kid, and I appreciate it more than I can tell you."

She turned to Jeff. "Where're you going?"

"I'm going along for kicks," he said jocularly.

"Oh ..." She turned pale and paused while a whole stunning reel passed before her eyes. Turning on her heel, she strode rapidly out of the trophy room.

Johnny cocked an eye at Jeff. "What did that mean?"

Jeff, a little pale himself shook his head. "Nothing probably."

"I wouldn't bet on it. Why don't you go see?"

Jeff's square jaw clamped shut. "I think I will."

He found her in the kitchen sitting at a table playing absently with a small paring knife and staring into space.

When he spoke she started. "Oh, Jeff ... I ... you scared me."

He sat in front of her and locked her in the grip of his eyes. "Larry ... you ran out a while ago. Why?"

She put a slender hand to her face and looked at him, her eyes dark with question. "I really don't know. Johnny seems so ... so, well, swashbuckling and capable ..." She shook her head. "No, that isn't it. You beat him one day. It's ..." She looked at him hard as though having difficulty focussing her eyes. She let go a fluttering sigh and shook her head slightly. "There's no use trying to tell you how I felt ... feel. Your going into that danger just flattened me. Jeff, tell me what ... Tell me why all of a sudden your being in danger frightens me, makes me weak."

"Why do you want me to tell you?"

She passed a hand over her eyes. "It's all so strange and sudden." She held up her head and looked at him squarely. "Jeff, do you suppose, after all this time I could just be seeing you as a man?"

"It could be," he said seriously. "Think it over and we'll go into it when I get back."

They loaded the weapons and ammunition on the *Snorter* and were about to depart when the lumbering figure of Ole Nielson appeared and waved to them to stop.

"Ay saw the gons," he said in his thick Scandinavian accent, "and ay coom. Where you gawing, Jaff?"

"A little trouble, Ole," said Jeff carelessly. "Just the thing for married men to stay out of."

"Ay gaw with you," he said stolidly.

Jeff's eyes narrowed with annoyance. "Ole, there's a good chance of getting knocked off in this deal. There's no need for you to go."

"Ay gaw," he said, not batting an eye.

"Let 'im go," snapped Elf. "We ain't overburdened with men and I seen Ole use a rifle onct. I ain't forgot it yet."

Jeff eyed the powerful hulking figure and nodded. "All right, Ole. You're a long time dead, remember."

Ole shrugged ponderously. "Ay don't be dad no longer as you."

CHAPTER THIRTEEN

JOHNNY was at the wheel and Jeff stood a little to the rear. "Jeff, were you ever at Renfrow's?"

"I went out there once through curiosity. Elf told me the bearing to take. It hasn't changed, has it, Elf?"

Elf, standing near the starboard rail shook his head. "Not 'less the island's done moved."

Johnny looked at the binnacle subconsciously, then into the leaden murk ahead. They were only carrying navigation lights.

A considerable time later Elf switched those off. "Don't want no lookout to git wind o' us atall."

Johnny motioned to Elf to take over. "You know it better than anyone else," he said. "Where'd be the most unsuspecting place to land?"

Elf sniffed at the chill damp wind and pondered for a moment. "Renfrow's ain't no bigger'n my island 'cept it's got a rocky middle and one side is straight up ... all but one place. Sand spit runs out a ways and we can circle and come in if we go slow." He angled the splintered bow of the *Snorter* away from dead ahead by ten degrees. "Usta be a trail sorta up the rock then ye stands on the highest point on the island. Buildin's down the slope near the beach. I wouldn't 'spect to find lookouts there."

"No lookouts anywhere," rumbled Ole surprisingly.

"How come?" asked Elf waspishly.

"If they ban expecting anybody they don' stop there in forst place. They think they all right now. Averybody gaw to bad."

Johnny laughed, letting some of the excitement he felt creep into it. "I hope you're right, Ole. It sounds logical."

It was more than that. It was prophetic. They tied the *Snorter* to a stunted tree by using a long hawser. Guarding against unwanted noise, they slowly mounted the rocky, unused trail to the rim and peered down at the dim outlines of trees and several buildings.

Johnny, whose skin had almost crawled off his bones at the prospect of making a landing, not knowing whether or not they would be greeted by a hail of machine gun bullets, felt relief sweep through his body. There were a few scattered dim lights but no movement could be seen.

The stillness was complete with only the dull boom of her surf pounding the rocks at their backs, impinging on their eardrums.

Johnny straightened up cautiously. "Since we don't know what we'll find or where or how many men there are, I have an idea. Suppose I go on across the island and find the boats. I'll set one afire and that should draw them out. Jeff, you yell and give them one chance to surrender, then … well, follow whatever is indicated. If anyone has a better idea, say so."

It appeared that no one did. "Just one thing," continued Johnny. "Mari might be here. For God's sake don't anyone shoot her."

Jeff said, "I think the three of us should stick pretty close together to keep from shooting each other. I've seen darker nights, but it doesn't have to be very dark to get mixed up. How'll you fire the boat?"

"I brought a bottle of gasoline along. Why?"

"If you get close enough to set it afire you'll be close enough to use this. Give me the bottle." He handed Johnny a small square block.

"What's this," said Johnny squinting in the dark.

"Triton block. It'll blow that boat to bits and there'll be a merry bonfire when the gasoline fires. It works like a hand grenade. It has a seven second fuse."

"What'll you do with the bottle?"

Jeff thought for a moment. "As soon as they rush toward the boat I'll set fire to something behind them and we'll have them between the two fires."

"Whut time is it," asked Elf.

"Two ten," said Johnny, looking at his wrist watch's luminous dial. "You in a hurry?"

"Nup. Jes' wanna be sure we git this thing done 'fore daylight. I don't wanna git caught out there in the sun."

Johnny took a ten minute lead and the others waited. Jeff, still but as tense as spring steel, Ole phlegmatic and nerveless, and Elf treating the whole operation with vast contemptuous calm.

Jeff stood up and made a motion with his hand. "Okay," he said quietly. "Let's load and lock now so the noise won't be heard." There were several soft metallic clicks as cartridges were fed into empty chambers, then they filed slowly down the slope toward the nearest of the lights.

Finding a good path, Jeff quickened his pace and, after some minutes walk, closed in on the nearest light. It proved to be a low shed-like building with low eaves and screened with coarse wire. There was a gasoline lantern hanging in the middle of the building beneath which a card game was going. One man lay on a cot apparently asleep. At the table was Erico Pucci, Griff, and two more men Jeff didn't know.

Evidently the bigger building was where Renfrow lived since this one was obviously a temporary barracks.

Jeff whispered low in Elf's ear. "Can you hit the bowl of that light?"

"Shucks ... nuthin' to it. I can shoot the mantle off if ye want."

"Just the bowl. Maybe it'll start a fire inside and ...

From the beach area came a dull boom and instantly the men were on their feet. "Where the hell did that come from," snarled Griff, tense and frightened.

No one answered him but the sudden lurid flame that sprang into being did and with one accord they ran out of the building and toward the beach.

Jeff pulled the stopper of the bottle and let the gasoline pour against the building and on the ground. When it was half gone he said quietly, "Okay Elf."

The Winchester lashed out a stinging report and for a moment it appeared that nothing would happen, but finally the spray from the escaping air and fuel reached the mantel and lit up with a soft explosion.

Jeff then dropped a match into the gasoline and they ducked away from the fire into the shadows of what appeared to be a small kennel or chicken house.

In a very few minutes it seemed that the whole island was red with the light of the fires; and men could be seen running aimlessly to and fro, trying to obey the incoherent orders of the now frantic Griff. They had gotten guns from some cache, there being several rifles, a submachine gun and at least one sawed off shotgun.

Jeff, still in the dark shadows, let go a clarion call. "Drop your arms and surrender. You're surrounded."

The men stood still for a moment trying to decide where the voice had come from. One threw down his rifle and Erico shot him through the chest with an automatic.

Jeff spoke one word. "Ole ..." Ole's hunting rifle crashed and Erico dug up sand.

"Who'll be next?" came the voice again and this time Griff, whose eyes had grown relatively used to the light, managed to locate them and screamed at the tommy gunner, throwing his own rifle to his shoulder.

The Winchester roared twice so fast that Jeff blinked when Griff and the sub-gunner both collapsed.

There was a ripping stutter farther around toward the fire on the water, and .45 caliber slugs whistled over their heads.

"That was Johnny," said Jeff and called out again. "Down those weapons or we'll blow you apart."

The remaining man threw his weapon down and prudently fell on his face.

The silence then was dead and oppressive with the only sound being that of the burning building. Then they saw Johnny herding three men toward them so they went to meet him, bringing their own prisoner along.

Johnny's face was white and strained and called to them. "Take over. I have a special job." And turning he raced back toward the big house.

Prudence told him it was foolhardy to charge the dim old house in the open, but he had heard a scream that tore his nerves to shreds. Only by superhuman will did he resist the urge to mow his prisoners down and hurl himself headlong into the house.

Around the house was a tall growth of bamboo and through this he charged like an elephant gone berserk. Two shots whistled by his ears and he stopped long enough to fill the window from which the flame had come with a hail of bullets firing from the hip. He tossed away the empty magazine and re-rammed another home, working the actuator to load the chamber and continued to the broad low verandah.

He dealt the door a fearful kick with his right foot and though the heavy door rocked and splintered he could tell by the axis of motion that it was barred. He loosed a burst where he thought the bar was and kicked again. This time it flew open but caution now took over and Johnny leaped aside not a second too soon to avoid both barrels of a shotgun fired at point blank range. With one hand he stuck the gun around the corner of the doorway and touched off a sweeping burst, hearing to his satisfaction a body fall heavily. Then with his flashlight he swept the hall and saw that it was empty. On the floor was the cadaverous figure of an old man, gaunt, grey with a hard bitter face and bush hair. He had fought his last battle.

The scream sounded again almost overhead and he took the creaky steps four at a time. He attempted to turn at the first landing, but tripped and fell headlong up the steps … which was all that saved his life. A shotgun roared and a heavy charge of buckshot bored into the plaster over him. With his face twisted with urgency and the need for accuracy, he touched the trigger and the gun hammered a rivetting song of death, outlining in the muzzle flame a tremendous woman holding a single barrel shotgun. She stiffened and staggered backward, then in a dying effort to recover tottered and fell headlong down the stairs raising dust by the violence of her fall.

He switched on the flashlight and picked out the figure of a slender girl crouched against the wall, her long, inky hair shimmering in the light.

"*MARI!*" His voice shook the walls as it tore itself from the very depths of his soul. It brought the girl to her feet where she hesitated a second giving his starving eyes their first look in centuries, it seemed, of the outrageous perfection of her curves from her smooth small ankles to the crown of her lovely head. Then, with a scream, filled with pent-up longing, she hurled herself into his arms.

There was restraint and silence aboard the *Snorter* that was hard to account for. The mission had been successfully completed. Griff's cruiser was astern, in tow. Aboard it were Griff, wounded but not dangerously, the bound captives of his group, and Elf, sitting on the damaged stern with his rifle in the crook of his arm, looking as though he'd rather enjoy some effort on the part of his passengers to make a break.

Johnny stood at the wheel and seemed to battle the *Snorter* through the waves at a speed that, at times, approached the danger point. At his feet, Mari crouched, half sitting, half kneeling. She was poetry in her ragged clothes that bared half her thighs and draped various shreds of gesture across the delicacy of her pointed breasts.

To Johnny she was the steam in a turkish bath, creeping back where she had always been—into every pore, every wrinkle and crack in his body and being. He inhaled her; he swallowed her. Her nearness, after all this time of longing, effectively stopped any possible speech. Yet, between them was a mighty thundering force demanding that they be alone. It lashed at them, urged on by the fiercest of all longings and reminded them of the time that had been lost. Now and again one or the other would try to still rigors that shook them from head to foot.

CHAPTER FOURTEEN

JEFFERY WICKWARE couldn't find Larry ... until she wanted him to find her. When he did, she did not have a stich of clothes on. The sight halted him dead in his tracks and his head seemed to spin crazily. He tried to speak, but only a dull meaningless croak came from his lips.

She came to him, her face wet with tears that had dripped upon the ivory globes of her breasts and by accident upon the rigid excited tip of each was a trembling gem that had never before and would never again find so rapturous a setting.

"I died a thousand times, Jeff," she said, her lungs struggling for air. "Then I knew and I wonder how I could have been so blind ... Jeff, get like me. Kill me with your love, Jeff, because I've never known it before. All I've known and tasted has been something to make this moment what I know it'll be."

He nodded and complied because he could not speak ... not the language of words, but in the language of love he soared upward and joined the ranks of masters whose names have thrilled millions. He could not match them in that but he did his best and combined all the love of millions into one gigantic flaming pyre that nearly consumed them by its ferocity, yet drew them to a land of peace and repleteful calmness they had never known but ever more would seek.